The Class Project Showdown

The Class Project Showdown

Rick Blanchette

Tyndale House Publishers, Inc.
Wheaton, Illinois

Books in the Choice Adventures series

Library of Congress Cataloging-in-Publication Data

Blanchette, Rick, date
  The class project showdown / Rick Blanchette.
    p. cm. — (Choice adventures series ; #10)
  Summary: The reader's choices determine the course of the
adventures of some junior high boys as they make decisions and moral
choices while working on a class project.
  ISBN 0-8423-5047-0
  1. Plot-your-own stories. [1. Schools—Fiction. 2. Adventure
and adventurers—Fiction. 3. Christian life—Fiction. 4. Plot-your-
own stories.] I. Title. II. Series: Choice adventures ; #10.
PZ7.B595C1 1992
[Fic]—dc20   92-30501

Printed in the United States of America

99 98 97 96 95 94 93
8   7   6   5   4   3   2   1

Jim, Willy, Sam, and Chris gazed at each other in disbelief. Jim looked at Pete and shrugged his shoulders. Pete lowered his head and said nothing.

Willy whispered to Chris, "It's a trick question."

Just when the boys were certain that no one would know the answer, a hand shot up from the front right side of the class.

"Yes, Sidney," Miss Vance said, "do you know the answer?"

"Yes, ma'am. The Civil War began and ended on the land of a man named McLean. The first major battle of the war was on and around his property near Bull Run Creek. The family moved to Appomattox, and Lee surrendered to Grant four years later inside McLean's home."

A chill went down Pete's back. Several "ooohs" and "wows" erupted throughout the room, and Chris, Willy, Sam, Jim, and Pete—the Ringers, as they called themselves—stared at one another with their mouths hanging open.

"That's correct, Sidney," Miss Vance said, smiling broadly. Sidney's answer had surprised her, pleasantly.

It had also surprised Pete Andersen—class brain—*unpleasantly*.

He stared over at Sidney. *Who is this kid?* Sidney was new to Madison Junior High, and Pete had scarcely noticed

2

him. Sidney was shy and quiet and had said little until now. In fact, just about everybody had scarcely noticed him.

Until now.

This could just be a fluke, Pete thought, trying to calm himself. *On the other hand, . . .* Pete was not one to take chances. He decided to keep a close eye on Sidney from now on. He glared in Sidney's direction.

"We only have ten minutes of class left, and I want to get you started on your group projects," Miss Vance said. She paused for a moment to let the chorus of groans die down. "The theme of the project is 'Community Awareness—What Millersburg Needs to Know.' Each group can decide exactly what it will report on, but you have to focus on something that affects Millersburg. Since there are twenty-four of you, we will divide into four groups of six. Now, to— Yes, Willy?"

"Miss Vance, can we pick our own groups?" Willy asked, still holding up his hand.

"Yes, you may."

"Yes!" Willy turned to Chris and gave him a high five before he lowered his hand.

"Before you get too excited," continued Miss Vance, "let me give you the details of the project. Each group is to write a thousand-word essay on its subject and make a formal presentation to the class. The presentation can be. . . ."

As Miss Vance droned on with the details of the assignment, Pete's mind wandered. He saw Sidney standing thirty paces away, motionless except for the fingers of his right hand, twitching nervously at the six-shooter hanging lazily in its holster. The dust blew and whistled between them as onlookers peeked out from the windows of the saloon and the general store.

"Draw," Pete said.

Suddenly—

". . . and it is due on Friday, the twenty-third, which is three weeks from today."

The room echoed with the sounds of pencils hitting desks and a muffled "Oh, man!" and a "No way!" A girl in the back pleaded, "Can't we have more time?"

Pete, having come back to reality, nodded his head and smiled coolly. *Perfect,* he thought to himself.

Miss Vance walked to her desk and skimmed through her calendar. She looked as if she was seriously thinking about moving back the due date.

Pete panicked. *No. No. Let it be impossible!* he thought, hoping for a chance to show off.

"Well, Melissa," she said, "I guess I could make the project due a week later, but then it would be too late for the group with the best grade to use the free circus tickets it's going to win."

Free circus tickets! Pete looked around at his classmates and then raised his hand, thinking fast. "Miss Vance, I think I can speak on behalf of the whole class when I say that three weeks is ample time for us to complete this challenging and fascinating assignment." He grinned widely, straight at Miss Vance, as the class nodded in agreement.

"I'm glad to see that you have all decided to accept this project . . . even if you did have to be bribed," she said, smiling. "You can have the rest of the class time to break into your groups. Monday we will take the first half of class to work on your topics and outlines. You can move around into groups now, but do it quietly."

Pete breathed a sigh of relief and clenched his fist in triumph. With a difficult project due in three weeks, the gang was bound to turn to him to save the day. Sidney would never take the lead in a group of his own, being new to the class.

The showdown had begun.

CHOICE

Turn to page 28.

Chris shrugged his shoulders and stood up. "Sorry, man," he said and then walked over to Jim and Sidney. Willy and Sam smiled these weak little sheep-eating grins and got up and joined their friends, who were no longer in Miss Vance's doghouse. Pete looked at them in total shock.

Miss Vance was pleased to see that most of the boys had finally obeyed her. "Well, now that we've got that all straightened out, take what little time there is left to start planning your projects."

When the bell rang, Pete really got it. His grade for the project was a zero, and he had to sit out in the hallway whenever the class worked on the projects. Talk about embarrassing! Miss Vance also called his parents, who were very disappointed in Pete's behavior. They even grounded him for a month, without letting him use the computer!

The other Ringers were surprised to find out that Sidney wasn't too bad of a kid. He was real quiet, even more so than Jim. They even managed to have some fun while working on their report and presentation. Their project, however, didn't win the circus tickets. Apparently their topic, the workings of 9-1-1, wasn't all that exciting, except to Pete, and he wasn't even there to enjoy it—he was in the hallway!

6

THE END

This didn't turn out so well for Pete, did it? To see what could have happened if the Ringers had worked with Sidney, turn back to the beginning and try other choices.

Or, turn to page 117.

It was Sidney who suddenly showed courage. "We have to go in. Aren't you dying to know what's in there?"

"Dying is a definite possibility," said Sam.

"Let's go in!" Willy put on a big smile. "We'll just have to check things out really close before we touch them."

Jim took another look inside the room and said, "I *would* like to find out what's there. What if there's something real important or—"

"Or valuable, like a chest of gold or jewels," imagined Willy out loud.

"OK." Chris gave in. "If you want to snoop around, we will. But nobody touches anything until we've thoroughly scoped it out."

With Sidney now in the lead, they cautiously entered the room. Sidney searched with the light, scanning a lot of crates that were stacked to the ceiling. The walls were covered with the same unfinished wood panels as the hallway. And directly in front of them was the crossbow.

As Sidney finished his scan, the beam of light fell upon the corner of a blanket that was behind a pyramid of crates. The gang slowly walked over to the blanket. It was covering something that made a long, not-too-high lump.

"What do you think's under there?" Willy asked.

"I don't know," Pete answered. "But is it safe to touch?"

8

Sidney examined the edges of the blanket, then the ceiling above and the crates next to it. "There don't seem to be any cords or traps or anything. I think it's safe."

"There's only one way to find out," said Willy. He stepped up to the blanket and said, "Stand back." Once the guys stepped several feet back, Willy edged back a bit and grabbed a corner of the blanket. "Keep the light on it, Sidney." With a deep sigh Willy gave a tug on the corner, and the blanket flew off the lump, raising a dust cloud.

In front of the boys was a pile of military articles, some of which were very unusual.

"Wow! I wonder who this stuff belonged to," said Sam.

"Maybe there's some identification in here," replied Chris.

"What are these?" asked Jim as he held up an object that looked like two leather bottles fastened at the bottoms by a leather and fur strap.

"Those are saddle holsters," Sidney answered. "I bet the guy who owned this stuff was an officer. Just look at the craftsmanship on the leather, and those caps at the pointy end are probably silver. My dad says that officers always had the fanciest weapons and stuff because they were usually rich."

"Here's his sword," exclaimed Willy. He pulled out the curved sword from the leather scabbard.

As he did so, the guys surrounded him and breathed "Wow!" They could hardly believe their eyes.

"Pretty fancy," said Willy, understating their awe. "Check out the end of the handle. There's a lion's head on it."

"That's an officer's sword," added Sidney. "They usually carried short sabers. See, that's only about two feet long. Hey! What's that paper over there?" Sidney moved behind Willy and picked up a piece of paper that was underneath a set of old saddlebags.

Chris and Pete looked over Sidney's shoulder as he held up the paper.

"It looks like some proclamation or something," Chris guessed.

"Yeah. And by the feathers and black tar stuck to it, I don't think the messenger was too popular," said Pete.

"No wonder. This is a request for volunteers for the *British* forces. It says that any Loyalist that wanted to enlist could join the British troops in Richmond." Sidney looked up at the Ringers. "Guess who signed it."

Both Chris and Pete were still reading, and their eyes raced to the bottom of the page. The other guys were trying to crowd in to get a look at the document.

Pete's eyes got really wide when he read the name: "General Benedict Arnold."

"The traitor?" asked Jim.

"Yeah. When his treason was discovered, he fled to the British forces and became a general against us. Around New Year's 1781, he captured Richmond and held it for a few days. He was really hated by Americans. People burned him in effigy and everything."

"Where's Effigy?" Sam asked. "Is it near Richmond?"

"It's not a place, nimrod," Pete answered with some laughter. "Sidney means that they burned a stuffed doll and pretended it was him."

Sam quickly nodded his head. "I knew that. I was just testing you."

"What we've got here is the all-time coolest, out of this world, get-an-*A*-and-go-to-the-circus social studies project!" Chris exclaimed, his voice cracking with excitement.

"I hear a swish," said Sam.

The guys gave each other high fives and cheered, celebrating their success. When the excitement died, Jim asked, "After our report, what do we do with it all?"

Chris spoke up immediately. "Let's split it up six ways and keep it."

"But doesn't this stuff," Sidney said, "really belong in a museum or collection somewhere?"

The boys had a problem.

CHOICE ⇒

If they decide to keep their treasure, turn to page 49.

If they donate it all, turn to page 102.

Since he liked computers and electronics, Pete was excited about Officer Gary's idea. And Jim always did wonder how all that stuff worked. Following Pete's lead, the gang scrunched into the police car and took the short ride to the police station. Willy was disappointed because Officer Gary wouldn't turn on the siren.

Once they were all inside the police station (which was in the basement of City Hall), they went to a conference room, and Officer Gary started a rather long, detailed description of the 9-1-1 system. He was only about a minute into his speech when Sam was completely lost. Sneaking out to get a drink of water seemed a whole lot better than being bored, so Sam quietly moved from his chair out into the hallway.

Suddenly he heard two men laughing. "Let's continue this in my office, Senator. There's more privacy there, if you know what I mean."

Wow! Sam thought. *Chief Brown and a senator. I wonder what they're talking about.* Once Sam heard the police chief's door close, he crept down the hallway and put his ear to the chief's door.

"Chief Brown, I'm sure you know how boys love to have fun. I'm sure you cut loose in your younger days, eh? I know I did." The senator paused to chuckle. Sam could hear Chief Brown laughing, too.

"That's true, Senator. That was a while ago, I'm afraid. But I'm sure you didn't come down here just to talk to me about our youth. What exactly can I do for you?"

"As you know, this is the year I'm up for reelection. And I've done a lot of good for our state, as you are aware. But . . . well, how should I put this? My son, Roger, has been, well, a little adventuresome lately. His mother's been ill, and I'm busy traveling and campaigning. There was no one else to watch the boy except for his grandmother, who happens to live in your fair community."

The senator paused, then his voice sounded very serious. "Roger has had several close calls with the police in D.C., but I've managed to take care of things—keep things quiet. But while he's here, he will be away from my protection. I've already made arrangements with Principal Jackson at the high school to take care of any embarrassing events that might occur at school. And now I'm asking you—"

Voices from down the hallway drowned out the rest of what the senator said. The voices got louder as they came toward Sam. Not wanting to get caught, Sam took a few steps away from the door and pretended to tie his shoelace. Judge Weber and Officer Cliff came around the corner laughing and talking. They walked right past Sam without even looking at him and then went up the stairs.

I hope I didn't miss too much, Sam thought as he crouched back down at Chief Brown's door.

As Sam listened, he heard the senator's voice say, ". . . some new cars, maybe even enough to get you started on a proper police station, not some dirty basement."

"Well, Senator, these things—" Again Sam was interrupted. A voice over the PA system asking Miss Garner to come to the information desk blared through the corridor.

"This never happens to James Bond," Sam growled as he threw an annoyed glance at the speaker in the ceiling.

Sam could again hear the chief when the announcement ended: "—to see a youth avoid serious problems. Of course I'll help you out with—what was that?" Chief Brown said as he jumped up from his desk.

Sam couldn't believe it. Of all the times to sneeze, he had to sneeze now! His sneeze was so strong that it knocked him off balance, causing him to crash into the chief's door. *What should I do?*

 **CHOICE**

If Sam decides to run away, turn to page 88.

If he stays, turn to page 113.

Wʰo?" Sam stopped and looked up at the church. "I really didn't think about that. It would have to have a name . . . to _be_ somebody, right?"

"Of course, he's probably been dead for at least fifty or sixty years, maybe longer," Chris stated. "And since he was locked in that room, there might be some mystery to how he died."

"Maybe he was murdered," Pete thought out loud.

"Let's go back and solve the case of the skeleton!" shouted Willy. "Who's goin' in with me?"

"Count me in," Chris said first.

"Me, too," Pete followed.

"I'll go," Jim said. "I'll get a flashlight from my grandpa's office and meet you upstairs."

Sam and Sidney looked at each other and swallowed hard. Sam said, "What do you say, Sidney? He's already dead. What can he do to us?"

"That's true. . . . OK, let's go. But only because finding a skeleton has got to be worth an _A_ on our project."

The gang wound its way back upstairs to a waiting Jim. He had a large silver flashlight in his hand and was shining it around the room.

"Who got an _A_ in health last year?" asked Jim. When Pete answered, Jim held the flashlight out to him and said, "You can check out the skeleton since you know the most about that stuff."

"Thanks," Pete said nervously. He took the light and slowly entered the room. When he located the skull with his beam of light, he motioned for the guys to follow him. Keeping the light on the head, Pete walked around it, looking at it but being very careful not to actually touch it.

What was that? Pete asked himself when a flash of light reflected back at him. He stooped down to take a closer look at the skull. Pete started laughing as he reached out and grabbed the head.

"You're sick, man!" yelled Sam.

"That's gross!" echoed Willy.

Pete stood up dramatically, held out the skull, and said, "Alas, poor Yoric. I knew him, Horatio."

"You are twisted, Pete," Chris groaned. "Have some respect for the dead, will ya?"

"I always wanted to play Hamlet. Relax," Pete casually said. "When we studied the body in health, does anyone remember seeing one of these attached to the bones?" He turned the skull so that the top of the head faced the group.

Their eyes widened as they looked at a metal loop at the top of the head.

"What we solved is the case of the missing medical skeleton!"

"Like in the doctor's office, Pete?" asked Jim.

"Yeah. Some report, huh?"

"I feel so stupid," Sam said, laughing. "Scared out of the church by some plastic and wire."

"Now that we have some light, should we get back to looking for something to do our report on?" Pete asked as

16

he tossed the skull up and down.

"Forget it!" Sidney said. "I'm not sticking around here. I'm gonna go watch TV."

"I'm with you," agreed Sam. "Real or not, that thing gives me the creeps. Let's come back tomorrow and try another room."

"OK, tomorrow then. But next time, Jim, when you get a key from your grandpa, make sure it isn't a *skeleton* key!" joked Chris.

THE END

Turn to page 117.

The paper says not to enter. Shouldn't we obey it?" Jim asked.

"Yeah. I'd hate to have anybody think I'm a traitor to the colonies," teased Sam.

"What would George Washington say?" Chris jokingly asked.

"I'd forgive you," Willy said.

Everyone laughed except Sidney, who didn't know that Willy's full name was William George Washington.

"C'mon, Jim," Pete said. "That notice was written more than two hundred years ago. It doesn't apply to us."

"Does the Bible apply to us?" Jim asked.

"Yes, but what's that got to do with this room?"

"The Bible was written thousands of years ago, and it still applies. But something written a couple of hundred years ago doesn't?"

"But that was written by God, and—"

"Before you guys get into a big argument, we can't get in even if we wanted to." Chris's observation silenced the group.

The door was quite thoroughly locked.

"Maybe there's a key around here somewhere," Sidney said. "If they locked the door, there has to be a key."

"At our house we keep an extra key above the door," offered Sam, aiming the flashlight around to look for a place where someone might have hidden a key.

"That's a great idea, Sam. I'll just grab this old box, put it by the door here, climb up on it, feel around the ledge for a key. . . ." As Pete jokingly searched, his hand came across something thin and made of metal. A puzzled expression crossed his face as he picked up a key.

" . . . And I'll find one," he finally said. Pete handed the rusty key to Chris and jumped off the box.

"Those colonists may have been patriotic, but they weren't too smart," Chris said. "Hiding a key above a door you don't want anyone to get into—"

"Hey!" Sam interrupted. "Watch what you're saying."

"Nothing personal, Sam. Sorry. We might as well see if this key works. You found it, Pete. Wanna try?"

"You bet." Pete took the key and tried it in the lock. He jiggled and wiggled the key without success. "Either this isn't the key, or the tumblers are as rusty as the key." He kept working the key, trying harder and harder to get it to turn. After several minutes and about a dozen offers from the others to try, they heard a *click*.

"We're in, guys," Pete said. "Everyone ready?"

They all nodded rapidly. Pete grabbed the black iron ring and pulled, but he didn't move the door. Trying again, he jerked on the door and almost pulled his arm out of its socket.

"Hinges are rusty," Sidney said. "Or maybe the frame shifted."

"Whatever happened, I need some help. Chris, Willy, Jim, grab on and help pull. Sam, you and Sidney stand out of the way, OK?"

Sam was the smallest of the guys and was usually left out of any "he-man" efforts wherever they were and whoever they were with. "Sure," he said, then added, "Here, Sidney. You can hold the flashlight."

The four guys clutched the door handle and at the count of three pulled with all their might. They grunted and groaned and gradually got the door open a crack. More pulling opened the door a little farther.

"It's getting easier," Pete said between breaths. "We've almost got it."

They gave one more hard tug, and the door swung open, throwing the boys backwards into a heap. As soon as the door opened wide, Sam and Sidney heard a *click* and a *twang* from the room, and an arrow *whirred* out the door and stuck in the wall opposite the doorway.

"Whoa! Somebody really didn't want us in there," an amazed Sam said when Sidney shone the light on the arrow.

Sidney stuck his head in the doorway, directing the flashlight around until he saw a crossbow. A rope was stretched across the room, one end tied to the trigger and the other tied to the door handle. "A booby trap," he said.

The four Ringers who opened the door were still on the floor. They stared at the arrow with their mouths wide open.

"That could've hit one of us," Chris slowly said.

"Not cool," Sam responded.

They got up, walked around the open door and gazed at the crossbow. Nobody moved.

"Is it safe to go in?" asked Jim.

20

"I dunno," answered Chris.

"If whoever wrote the warning was serious, and it seems they were, I bet there are more traps set up—to make sure that no one who enters leaves." Pete looked again at the arrow. "Anyone want to take the chance?"

CHOICE ⟹

Are the Ringers on the verge of another great discovery? If you think the gang should take the risk and go in, turn to page 7.

On the other hand, what if it *is* dangerous? If they decide to play it safe and leave, turn to page 36.

The Ringers and the girl (who they discovered was Margaret Grant, a freshman at "Stonewall" High) got to the station just before Officer Gary and Roger.

When Officer Gary came in, he was not his usually friendly self. He growled at Roger, "Get in here, and stop draggin' your feet!" To the officer at the front desk he shouted, "I'm gonna book this punk as soon as the chief gets done with him. Have the paperwork ready!" Then he pulled Roger down the hallway and into Chief Brown's office.

After a couple of minutes Officer Gary came out of the chief's office with a big smile. He approached the group and then called Margaret aside. They spoke for several moments. Margaret shook Officer Gary's hand and then she left, but not before hugging each of the Ringers.

"What's goin' on, Officer Gary?" Sam asked. "Why isn't she pressing charges, and why are you smiling?"

"And," Chris asked, "is Chief Brown going to let Roger go?"

"To answer your questions: The young lady is not pressing charges because she just wants to go home and forget about this. I changed moods because I was only acting to be angry. And Chief Brown will let Roger go, but only after we put a good scare into him."

"What?" everyone asked.

"Is that why the senator was here? To get his son out of trouble!" Sam was definitely mad.

22

"Calm down, Sam. Let me explain. Technically we can't keep him in jail if no one charges him with anything. Senator Lee was here—Oh, I get it. You think Chief Brown was supposed to protect Roger, right?" The gang nodded. "It's the opposite. Senator Lee said that his son was getting into too much trouble and always expected his dad to bail him out. So the senator asked us to really give it to Roger hard as soon as he caused any problem. He wanted to scare him before he really got into anything serious. The chief will yell at him, I'll 'book' him, then we'll put him in a cell until his dad comes, which will probably be several hours."

"You mean there was no bribe?" Sam said, disappointed.

"A little scheming, yes. A bribe, no way."

As they were walking home from the station, Jim realized that their project was due in two days, and they had nothing done.

The next two nights were spent throwing together a report about 9-1-1. Pete and Sidney were right; there was no problem with them coming up with an essay. Pete didn't even mind having another "brain" around, especially since he would have had to do most of the writing if Sidney wasn't around.

Unfortunately the project was supposed to be more than just a written report. The other Ringers worked on the visual aids. When Sam looked at their finished poster, he said, "We'd better call 9-1-1. This thing is going to need mouth-to-mouth CPR." The gang tried, but because Pete and Sidney had the only notes, several steps were not included, others were misspelled, and many more were totally wrong. The kids in the class enjoyed the presentation all right, but mainly because they laughed a lot.

"Hey! Is that a picture of an amoeba?" asked Joey Skinner, the class clown. While Joey was trying to be funny, Willy did have to admit that the poster looked more like an amoeba than a circular flowchart.

And when Sam read, "The police are alerted to the emergency," Jim reluctantly pointed to the next step, which read, "Police get doughnuts." Even Miss Vance couldn't help but laugh out loud.

Somehow the guys managed to get a *C*-minus on their project. While Jim, Pete, and Sidney were upset that they didn't get a better grade, the other Ringers were disappointed because they didn't win the circus tickets.

"We can still go to the circus, right?" Jim asked.

"I guess, but it won't be as fun since we didn't win tickets," Chris whined.

"We didn't win tickets," Sidney said, "but no one said we can't win stuff at the midway, right?"

The Ringers perked up. "Yeah! They always have cool prizes. I'm gonna win one of those big stuffed bears—for my sister, guys!" Willy finished after several strange looks from his friends.

They all left school that day talking about the prizes they would win at the circus midway. What actually happened at the circus, though, is another adventure.

THE END

Turn to page 117.

How 'bout this, Jim," Chris said. "We split into groups of two and take turns spying on the senator's son. We could do it just for a week or so. If something happens, we can do our report about it—kinda like investigative reporting. If it turns out to be a waste of time, we can always do the 9-1-1 thing. Sound fair?"

Jim looked at the eager faces of the Ringers and the pleading eyes of Sidney. He couldn't let his friends down. "OK, I guess we can do it, but just for a week. Oh, there's one more condition—I get to be James Bond!"

"You? James Bond? 007? Why not *me?*" asked Pete. "After all, Bond is a genius, right?"

"Hey! What about me?" demanded Willy. "007 is a brave, daring guy, just like me."

Jim answered, "Because I said it first, that's why me."

Sam smiled a devious grin as he spoke in his best Bond voice, "Gentlemen, all your arguing is useless. I'm Bond, James Bond. The reason is quite simple: I'm the only one here with trick gadgets."

"What?" they all said.

"I see you've underestimated me, my good men. I am armed with . . ." He paused dramatically as he reached inside his jacket pocket. Pulling out a thin object, he gave a wicked laugh. *"Ha!* A George Washington squirt pen! Anyone attempting to be James Bond, other than myself, shall find himself drenched!"

All the guys laughed. Most of them had already lost or forgotten about the squirt pens they'd bought in Washington over the summer.

Pete quickly changed tactics. "That's OK. You go ahead and be 007. I'd rather be Q. He's the real brains behind Bond anyway!"

"What about me?" Willy asked.

"I know," Chris immediately offered, "you can be Moneypenny!"

"Oooh! That was so funny I forgot to laugh! Let's just eat our ice cream so we can go bag another senator."

"What do you mean, Willy?" Sidney was confused. "Where did the *other* senator come in? Did I miss something?"

"Another day, another adventure. Someday we'll show you the newspaper clippings."

The Ringers divided into three groups: Jim and Sidney; James "Sam" Bond and Q "Pete"; and Chris and Willy (who very soon made the others stop calling him "Moneypenny"). They all went with Zeke and his friend Shorty to see where Roger Lee lived. He was staying with his grandmother, whose house was only a few blocks away from the Freeze. Shorty described Roger as "mega tall, with the most egregious red hair." The Ringers were glad to know that he'd be easy to spot in a crowd.

The next week was spent following Roger around everywhere—to the movies, the mall, friends' houses, and even the Freeze. Sitting in the Freeze eating banana splits turned out to be the best part of their undercover work, since standing in the cold playing spy got old real quick. What was even worse than freezing was the fact that Roger hadn't even done anything to get in trouble.

There was one incident that Sam managed to get on film, though. Roger and his friends were in the Millersburg Public Library when old Miss Cratchett came along and shushed them. But someone getting shushed by the librarian, they realized, was not exactly circus ticket–winning investigating.

One week of sneaking around turned into two and then into two and a half, since none of the gang, except Jim, wanted to give up.

"Listen, our report is due in a couple of days, and we haven't done any work on it yet. My grandparents will kill me if I don't do good in school here. Let's just spend the rest of our time working on the 9-1-1 report and forget about this."

"C'mon, Jim, one more day. If nothing happens, we'll work on that report tomorrow. If we catch Lee and Chief Brown lets him off the hook, then we've got the best report ever, and maybe our report will even get in the paper for exposing the thing."

"Sam's right," Sidney urged. "Pete and I could come up with a report in a few hours; it's pretty easy to do. But this opportunity may not come up again. Let's do it this afternoon, please?"

The gang kept nagging Jim until he gave in. "OK, but I'm just going to do it until dinner. If you want to follow him until curfew, you can. I'm gonna start on our report!"

After school they were on their way to "Stonewall"

High when they heard a girl call out for help. They looked around and saw a familiar red head disappear around a corner into an alley; then they heard another "Help! Stop it!"

"Let's check it out, guys!" Chris whispered kind of loudly, then led the group to the corner where Roger had vanished. "Take a look! You won't believe it!" Chris whispered, this time much quieter.

The Ringers gasped at what they saw. There in the alley was Roger Lee holding a girl who was struggling to get away from him.

"What do we do?" asked Willy.

"I've got my camera here," Sam said. "I can try to take a picture of this. That way we'll have some proof if Chief Brown says nothing happened."

"OK," Chris agreed. "Jim, Sidney, you guys run and get Officer Gary. He'll know what to do. Hurry up!"

Sidney and Jim took off toward the police station at a dead run. As the Ringers waited and watched around the corner, the girl was still wrestling with Roger, but now she was crying.

"Boy, I wish I could hear what he was saying!" Pete whispered.

"Yeah," Sam added, "and I would like to get a better picture. Hey Q, whaddaya say we sneak up closer?"

CHOICE

If Bond and Q creep in closer, turn to page 92.
If they all wait for Officer Gary, turn to page 66.

Immediately, kids ran from their desks to meet their friends and get into groups. The Ringers met at Chris's and Willy's desks in the back of the room.

The Ringers were that group of five boys and sometimes two girls who hung around Millersburg together—Willy, Chris, Sam, Pete, Jim, Jill, and Tina. They got their name from Mr. Whitehead, the new (well, retirement-age new) pastor of Millersburg Community Church, when they discovered some secret passages in the bell tower of the church. Even before Mr. Whitehead came, his sister, Chris and Willy's Sunday school teacher, had been fond of telling them, "Remember to be Ringers." A Ringer, you see, is a person who closely resembles someone else. It was her way of reminding them to be like Jesus.

The Ringers were glad to get to work together because they were already friends. They were also glad because that horrid Sharon Rasmussen didn't ask to join their group. The last time she worked with the Ringers, all she did was make goo-goo eyes at Chris. The guys teased him about that for a month. But all their present gladness was spoiled when Sam said, "Hey, there's only five of us. We need six."

They scanned the room to see who wasn't in a group. In a few moments, it became obvious that the only person sitting by himself was Sidney Knox.

Jim timidly said, "We could ask Sidney."

Pete suddenly felt a chill, and choked. Sidney? In *his* group?

Chris, Sam, Willy, and Pete stared at Jim as if he had green antennae growing out of his forehead.

"The new kid? I don't know," Chris said.

Pete's heart was racing at five hundred miles an hour. "No way!" he suddenly snapped. "He's a show-off. Always answering those tough questions. Forget it."

The rest of the guys were startled. "Whoa, Kimosabe!" said Sam. "Normal, serene Pete Andersen doth protest too much, foaming at the mouth and kicking buckets!"

"Chill, Ramirez," Pete snapped.

Jim figured he knew what Pete was thinking. "I was new when I first came, and you guys didn't lock me out. I think we should ask Sid to join us. Besides, what else can we do?"

"Well," Willy suggested, "we could ask Miss Vance if we can have just five in our group."

"Five. Let's do it," Pete ordered.

CHOICE ⇒

If Pete has his way and they try to get out of it, turn to page 55.

If the gang vetoes Pete's order and invites Sidney to join their group, turn to page 77.

30

I've only been in a church once, but I guess we could go there," Sidney said.

"Only once?" the Ringers shouted.

"Yeah, once . . . when my mom was killed a few years ago."

There was an awkward silence. No one knew exactly what to say, so they said nothing.

"Sorry to hear about that," Sam finally said.

"She was coming to pick me up from a friend's house when this dog ran out into the road. She swerved and missed the dog, but she hit a tree. Dad and I get along pretty good now. . . . Let's get going, OK?"

"Sure," Chris said. "Last one there's a Klingon!"

Chris started running down the school's parking lot toward the church, with the other Ringers and Sidney close behind. When they reached Capitol Community Church, the Ringers were amused by Sidney's reaction to the building.

"Wow! This is pretty old." Sidney looked up to the bell tower, then to the stained-glass windows above the main doors. "How long has the church been here?"

"I'm not sure," Jim said. "I know it was built before the Revolution, but I don't know when. I bet Grandpa knows."

"This gives me an idea for our project. Why don't we

do it about this church? A place this old has got to have some interesting history, right?"

"You can say that again, Sidney!" Chris said, laughing.

"But don't!" Sam added. The Ringers all groaned, except Willy, who gave Sam a high five.

"We hang out here all the time," Willy said. "It's cool with me if we do it for a grade. This is gonna be *fun.*"

"I think we should hit the upstairs first," Pete said.

"No way! I say we check around the basement. After running here from school, the last thing I wanna do is climb a bunch of stairs." Sam was still catching his breath.

"You got that right," agreed Chris. "All in favor of the basement?"

CHOICE⇐

If the gang decides to check out the upstairs, turn to page 107.

If they search the basement, turn to page 45.

Several minutes later Jim returned. He was swinging a large, rusty key from a long chain. "Grandpa says this is the only key he has. It should work in all these old doors."

"Do they only have one lock here?" asked Willy.

"No," Chris answered, "it's probably a skeleton key."

"What's a skeleton need a key for?" joked Sam.

"Maybe for when his *mummy* locks him out of the house," Willy joked back. All the guys groaned—except Sam, who exchanged a high five with Willy.

"Which room do we want to try?" Jim asked.

Chris answered, "The one on the left."

"Any special reason?" questioned Jim as he inserted the key into the lock.

"Moe told us to."

"Who's Moe, Chris?"

"Moe? You know, Eenie, Meenie, Minie, *Moe.*"

"I'm glad you put some serious thought into the choice." The lock clicked when Jim turned the key. As he opened the door, he asked, "Who wants to be first?"

Everyone looked into the room. It was dark, except for a thin beam of light from a small circular window near the ceiling. Throughout the room were indistinguishable shapes that were covered with drop cloths.

This is pretty spooky, thought Pete. So he said, "Sidney, since you're new, you may have the honors."

"Uh, well, . . . sure. OK, if no one else actually wants to go first." He looked at the Ringers, who shook their heads. Sidney stepped into the doorway and felt along the wall for a light switch. After a few moments he gave up and tried along the other side of the door. "There's no switch. Does this room have electricity?"

"It should," Jim answered.

"Maybe there's a light on the ceiling. You know, with a pull string hanging down. Why doesn't someone find it?" asked Willy.

"I'll check for it," Sidney volunteered. "Can you guys feel around for a lamp or switch or something?"

Slowly they entered the room. Sidney carefully walked, arms stretched upward, searching for a chain or string. The Ringers edged along the walls, feeling for a wall switch and groping at the covered items stacked throughout the room.

"I can't find anything," Sidney complained. "How about you?"

"Just boxes," said Chris. "Anyone else find a light?"

"I think I found a lamp, but I don't know why you need one. You can see me just fine." Sam had been standing so that his face was in the beam of light from the window and was in front of a tall, thin covered object. "Let me pull this tarp off and see what we have."

Sam tried uncovering the item, but the drop cloth was caught on something. He yanked really hard, and the cover flew off. But as the cloth came off, the object tipped over toward Sam. Once its path crossed the light beam, Jim screamed, "Aaaargh! It's a body!"

34

Sam was tangled up in the tarp when the object fell against him and knocked him over. When he looked to see what fell, he stared right into the eye sockets of a skeleton, its jaw hanging open as if it were laughing at Sam.

"Get it off me!" shrieked Sam. "Help!"

As he struggled to get loose, Sam kicked off the skeleton, which broke apart as he did so. The head rolled across the floor and hit Sidney's feet. Sidney and the other Ringers hadn't been able to see what was going on in the dimly lit room. Sidney looked closely at the human head that was beside him, jumped back, and took off running out the door and down the stairs. He was quickly followed by five panic-stricken Ringers.

They gathered at the base of the stairs outside the church and regrouped.

"What happened back there?" Chris asked.

"It was a . . . a skeleton! A body fell on me when I pulled on the drop cloth."

"Are you sure it was a skeleton?" Willy asked. "That's too weird to find in a church."

"Yeah, it was," Sidney said. "The head rolled and hit my feet! Man, that's the last church I ever go in." He turned to start home.

"Where you goin'?"

"I'm not going back in there, Chris. Dead people aren't my idea of a fun time!"

"I agree. Let's get outta here." Sam had begun walking away, too.

"Don't you want to find out *who* it is?" Pete asked.

CHOICE ⇒

If the boys go back in to investigate, turn to page 14.

If they don't, turn to page 59.

36

This'll be great! Let's go!" Willy yelled.

Everyone else just looked at him.

Chris gave a frown and said, "Chill, Wild Man. No school project is worth . . . *that!*" Chris pointed back to the arrow.

"Yeah," agreed Pete. "We have the whole weekend to come up with a topic."

"And there's probably a ton of things to do it on," said Sidney.

"Or we could always come back, maybe ask Pastor Whitehead for some help." Willy offered. "I guess I'm just getting carried away. This is way cool, and I do want to win those circus tickets."

"We'll still get the tickets," Jim assured Willy. "Between the six of us, we've got enough brains to get a great grade, no matter which topic we choose."

Suddenly Sam started counting in a whisper. He stopped at four, thought a moment, and then said, "Yeah, I think that's enough."

"Enough of what?" asked Willy.

"I was counting brains. I think we have enough."

"You're unplugged," said Chris, shaking his head. He looked back into the room and said, "Help me close this door, Willy. And then let's get out of here."

"OK, but I can't wait to come back and find out what's in there."

THE END

Willy may have to wait to see what's in the room, but you don't. To discover the mystery, turn to page 7.

Or, turn to page 117.

The Ringers knew they were beaten.

"OK, Miss Vance, we'll ask him over here," Chris said.

"That's a good decision, boys." Saying that, Miss Vance headed back to her desk.

"Now who goes over there to ask him?" Willy asked, hoping it wasn't going to be him.

"Why not have Jim do it?" Pete said shortly. "After all, he's the one who wanted him in our group anyway."

"I don't understand what the problem is," Jim said sharply. "You guys accepted me and Tina when we moved here to stay with our grandparents. We got along great. Besides, God wants us to be nice to Sidney."

Willy looked confused. "How do you know?"

"My grandpa was reading to us from Ephesians last night, and he read a verse that said something like we should be kind and merciful to others because God was like that to us when he saved us."

"I'll look it up. I've got a Bible here," Sam said as he reached under his desk for his books.

An intimidating voice from behind Sam said, "A Bible? In school? What a goody-two-shoes geek!" The voice belonged to Norman Bluto, the school bully.

"Yeah, a Bible," replied Sam, pulling out a leather-bound book from the stack by his feet. He turned and smiled at Norman and said, "We're just gonna look at something from the book of Ephesians. Do you want to read along?"

The Ringers were amazed at Sam. Where did he find the guts to stand up to Norman Bluto? Did he have a death wish? Was he insane? They wondered what would happen next and if their teacher would let them go visit Sam in the hospital.

But the unexpected happened. Norman didn't pulverize Sam. He didn't even yell or tease Sam. Instead, a puzzled look crossed Norman's face, probably because no one had ever *not* been frightened of him. And he wasn't sure how to respond to someone offering to let him see a Bible. All Norman managed to say was a mumbled, "No, no thanks." Then he turned back to join his group, which was just as amazed as the Ringers at the incident.

"Phew!" Jim said. "See what happens when we're nice to people? I'm gonna ask Sidney over here while you guys look up that verse. I think it was toward the end of chapter 4."

Jim walked across the room to Sidney, who was looking really lonely. Jim remembered how lonely he was when he first came to Millersburg. He didn't have any friends until Willy and Chris met him in the old church. Now he couldn't imagine not having the Ringers as his friends.

"Hey, Sidney. I'm Jim, and we want to know if you want to work on the project with us."

Looking first at Jim and then the Ringers, Sidney said, "I don't know. I mean . . . well, gee, I guess so. . . ."

"I know what it's like to be new. My sister and I moved here a little while ago from Brazil. It took us a while to get used to this area."

"Wow! Brazil," Sidney said with eyes wide open.

"That's pretty far away. Don't you miss home?"

"Yeah," Jim admitted. "Especially my parents—we're staying with my grandparents. But it's not so bad here, except it gets a lot colder than I'm used to. This is only October, and I'm freezing already! Well, come on. You gotta meet my friends. They're all great."

When Jim and Sidney got back to the Ringers, the guys had just finished reading Ephesians 4:32.

"Isn't it incredible how there's always something in the Bible to help us out?" Chris pointed out.

"Sidney said he'd work with us, guys."

"Jim, that's great," answered Chris, hoping the others would follow his enthusiastic lead.

Sure enough, Willy didn't disappoint him. Willy put a big smile on and said, "Sidney, do you know why the skeleton didn't cross the road?"

"Uh, I don't know. Why?"

"Because he didn't have any *guts!*"

Willy waited for the groans, and everyone obliged.

"You don't have it, Willy," Sam said, shaking his head. Then turning to Sidney he said, "Willy thinks he's cool, but he's really quite feverish."

Willy poked him.

Sam flinched and shot back, "The truth hurts, Kimosabe."

Pete interrupted. "Between me and Sidney, we should have those circus tickets all sewn up."

Turning to Sidney, Chris asked, "Say, how did you know the answer to Miss Vance's question?"

"Yeah," Willy added, "we thought it was a trick question."

"I read about it. My dad taught history at West Point, and I went through his books all the time. Military history is my hobby, I guess."

"Hey! Jill's hobby is history and stuff. She's my cousin and visits us a lot. Pete here," Chris said, noticing that Pete still wasn't into the spirit of friendliness, "his hobby is electronic things and computers. There's nothing about that stuff he doesn't know."

"I wish I could figure that out," said Sidney. "Maybe you could show me how to work my dad's computer sometime. He tries to teach me, but I keep erasing and losing a lot of his files somehow."

"It's all very simple," explained Pete. "I guess I could help you out." Pete suddenly remembered that Sidney was his competition for "class brain," so he quickly added, "That is, if I can find the time."

Chris looked at the clock. "Speaking of time, looks like school's about over. Wanna meet at the Freeze and plan our project?"

"I dunno, Chris. You know I don't like ice cream," Willy joked.

Sam burst out laughing. "Fine, then you can have a squid burger." Willy shot back, "That's real funny . . . *not!*"

CHOICE

Turn to page 115.

42

Get real! The Ringers would never turn their back on an adventure. Especially if doing so means having to work on a boring homework project.

CHOICE

Turn to page 23.

When the gang reached the Freeze, they sat in their usual seats and ordered six Independence Splits—bananas with a scoop each of strawberry, vanilla, and blueberry ice cream; strawberry topping; whipped cream; red, white, and blue sprinkles; a cherry, and a sparkler.

When Betty brought out the bodacious ice-cream creations, she informed the boys of the new rule: "No one gets served an Independence Split until he sings 'Yankee Doodle.' OK, fellas, hit it!"

The Ringers sang a loud, off-key version of "Yankee Doodle," with Sidney joining in once he was sure it wasn't a prank. When they finished singing, everyone in the Freeze clapped and whistled, causing the guys to sink down in their chairs in embarrassment . . . except for Sam, who bowed.

As soon as the people went back to their conversations, the boys started planning their project. Talking while they ate, they shot down one idea after another.

"Everything exciting is in D.C.," Pete complained. "Millersburg is boring!"

"Yeah. Officer Gary's offer is starting to look like a great idea," Chris said.

"I just don't know . . . ," Pete said as he shoveled some more banana split into his mouth, "mwha Mish Vansh mwansh?"

"That's OK, Pete. We don't know what you just said!"

Pete took a few more chews and then swallowed. "I said I don't know what Miss Vance wants. Some public service thing? An exposé?" Pete scooped up another gob of banana split and stuffed it into his mouth.

"There's probably plenty of stuff to do our project on, but now everything seems—Pete? What's wrong?"

While Jim was talking, Pete had suddenly turned red and was making gagging noises. He dropped his spoon and clutched at his throat.

"Pete! Are you OK? Are you choking?" called Chris.

Pete frantically nodded.

Chris stood up and yelled, "Our friend's choking! Can anyone help him?"

Sidney started to move, but then sat still again.

Pete kept choking.

"Please, can someone help Pete?" Willy shouted.

What should I do? Sidney asked himself. He began to panic as he tried to remember the CPR classes he had taken a year before. He had never actually had to use CPR on anybody in a real emergency, and now Pete was choking. His heart beat faster and faster as he tried to decide what to do.

CHOICE ➡️

If Sidney helps Pete, turn to page 105.

If he doesn't, turn to page 98.

Everyone raised his hand, even Pete, who was now having second thoughts about climbing all those stairs.

"Our Sunday school room might be a good place to start," suggested Chris. "We can use it for our project headquarters."

The boys slowly found their way downstairs to their room, stopping occasionally to show Sidney some secret entrances and explain something unique.

"My great-aunt taught in this room, Sidney," Jim said. "She died about a year before I came here from Brazil, so I didn't really know her."

"The room is just like she had it," Pete said. "The blackboard's in the same place, and even those ugly statues are still here."

Pete pointed toward a wall of built-in bookcases. On top of the oak cases were several white ceramic figurines that were definitely ugly, but two centuries ago they were "all the rage," as Miss Whitehead constantly reminded the boys. The men wore powdered wigs and looked to be dancing the minuet with ladies wearing dresses with big poofy skirts.

"Hey guys! Guess what I found," Willy called from the room's supply closet.

"A secret tunnel?" guessed Chris.

"Something better." Willy held up a small, bright

green object. "My superball I lost last Sunday. It must've rolled in here after it bounced off Sarah's Bible."

Sam laughed, remembering their out-of-control game of catch before class started. "Toss it here, Willy." Once he caught it, Sam called "Catch, Chris" and threw the ball.

Chris looked up, but too late. The superball hit Chris on the forehead, ricocheted to the top shelf of one of the bookcases, and thudded back and forth up there before finally losing its bounce.

"Why didn't you catch it? You almost broke those statues."

"No way! Those things are too gross to break. Besides, Sam, *you* threw it!"

"Well, whoever threw it, will *one* of you guys get my superball? I really need it. It drives Zeke nuts when I bounce it off the walls while he's studying—and he's had it too easy this week."

Zeke was Willy's older brother, whose real name was Clarence. He was a freshman at George Mason University.

"Don't blow a gasket, Willy," said Sam. "I'll get it. Wanna give me a hand?"

"Sure," Willy answered. Then Willy started clapping.

"That's so funny I forgot to laugh. Forget it! I'll do it without you."

Sam climbed the built-in bookcase, using the shelves like rungs of a ladder. Once he was about three feet off the floor, he began looking for the ball.

"Man! It's gnarly up here. There's dead bugs, cobwebs, and some mongo dust bunnies."

The guys glanced at each other and stifled giggles. They all mouthed, *"Dust bunnies?"*

"I don't see the ball up here. It might be in one of the other sections." Sam was scooting over on the shelves when he lost his footing. He reached for something to hold on to, but the only thing available was one of the ugly statues. He grabbed it, then realized that not only would the statue not hold him up, but he'd probably break the statue when he landed. But rather than fall, amazingly the statue moved only an inch and held Sam. While Sam was hanging there, he heard a rumbling sound and felt himself moving. "Earthquake!"

"Wrong coast, Einstein," Chris yelled over the roar. "You found a passage."

Sure enough, Sam quickly climbed down and took a look into a hidden passage. "The statue must have been a secret lever."

"I'll run and get a flashlight," Jim volunteered. "Don't start without me."

He returned a few moments later with the church's flashlight. "Should we let Sam lead? After all, it's his discovery."

"Sure," everyone agreed. The gang had learned the lesson that whoever was first in a dark tunnel was usually the one to trip, fall, bump into things, and get cobwebs wrapped around his head. Going first wasn't all it was cracked up to be.

"I'll take that," Sam said with a mock smile as he grabbed the flashlight from Jim and entered the tunnel.

The passage led forward for about ten feet before it turned left. Immediately after the turn were some very steep stairs that led below the basement. At the bottom of the staircase the hall turned left again. They followed this hallway until they could go no farther—the tunnel ending with a large, wooden door.

"Wow!"

"Excellent!"

"This looks like one of those doors in the swash-buckler movies," Willy said.

"Yeah. Like a castle dungeon. Check out the stone doorway, this big iron ring for the handle, the—what's that? Sam, put the light back there a minute! It looks like there's a note nailed to the door." Sidney stepped up to the door and carefully uncurled a piece of paper that was nailed to the door at an adult's eye level.

The paper read:

> *WARNING!*
> *We entreat ye not to enter this Room lest ye*
> *foul yourself with Treasonous Refuse. Open*
> *this Door and ye Prove yourself an Enemy to*
> *Gen. Geo. Washington and the Government of*
> *the United States of America.*

Those who could, whistled. Those who couldn't, said "Wow!"

"That sounds pretty serious. What should we do?" Sidney asked, after everyone had a chance to read the notice.

CHOICE ➤

If they ignore the warning and decide to go in, turn to page 17.

If they don't go in, turn to page 52.

I don't think it *has* to go to a museum," answered Pete. "Do you guys remember in sixth grade when that man spoke to us dressed up as a Minuteman? He had a lot of things from the 1700s."

"Didn't he have stuff like canteens, and cannon balls, and bullets?" asked Willy, trying to remember.

"Yeah," Chris replied, "and he even had a rifle and a couple of pistols. If he can have that stuff, we can have this."

"OK. I agree about the common items," Sidney said, giving in. "I'd kind of like to keep something, too. For my dad. But this letter from Benedict Arnold is too important for us to keep, right?"

"You're right about that. After the report we should give it to somebody. Maybe the Millersburg Historical Museum."

"Or, Sam, what about the history department at Mason U? My grandpa took me and my sister there a few weeks ago. They've got a lot of neat things there already."

"That's a great idea, Jim," Sidney said. "My dad can take us there and introduce us to the head of the department."

After arguing for fifteen minutes about how to get started, they decided to pick out which items they wanted and then do the research about whatever they chose.

Willy immediately picked the short saber and tried to put on the scabbard. The rest of the guys couldn't help laughing at Willy as he got tangled up in the straps. After finally figuring out that one strap went around his waist and the other around his shoulder, he looked at the guys, smiled weakly, and asked, "Did anyone else want this?"

"You keep it, Willy. Besides, I don't think you'll be able to get it off," joked Chris.

"Let's see what's in the saddlebags," Sidney said as he picked up the large, brown leather bags. "They sure are heavy."

Lifting up one of the flaps, Sidney found several small personal objects: a folding knife and fork set, a straight razor, an empty tinder box, and a leather wallet with the name *Capt. Albert Westfield* printed on it.

"You see? I told you he was an officer," Sidney reminded them when he read the name.

The other pouch contained two all-metal flintlock pistols and two brass spurs. They picked the items they wanted and then headed over to Sidney's house to plow through his dad's military books.

When they gave their report, the details about their possessions were interesting, but the thing that amazed the class was Benedict Arnold's proclamation. With Sidney's dad's help, they were able to include in their report a good guess at how the events happened.

"When Arnold's troops captured Richmond, he sent this enlistment notice dated January 5, 1781. When the messenger was caught by patriots, they probably took his possessions, tarred and feathered him, and sent him back toward Richmond. Then they locked everything in the secret room at the church so no one could take anything that belonged to the hated enemy."

Their theory about these events was good enough to earn them an *A* and the circus tickets. And when they donated General Arnold's letter to the university, the Millersburg newspaper featured an article about the gang's discovery and the university's collection of Revolutionary War documents.

Sidney was nervous when they were interviewed, but Willy reassured him, "Relax, man. This stuff happens to us all the time."

THE END

Turn to page 117.

I don't think we should," Jim said. "I mean, the sign says not to."

"The question isn't if we *should;* it's if we *can.* The door's locked, and we don't have a key," Chris complained.

"Would your grandpa have a key to this room?"

"I don't think so, Sidney. He might not even know about this room. Besides, he was leaving when I went up for the flashlight."

"Can we ask him about it?" Sam asked. "If he doesn't have a key or anything, maybe he can tell us something about what might be in there."

"Let's interview him about the whole church. Teachers like to see quotes from interviews. They're called 'primary sources.'" Pete looked over at Sidney to make sure he was impressed with Pete's knowledge of the ins and outs of report writing.

Sidney nodded in agreement. "And when we interview him, we should tape record it and use bits and pieces for our presentation."

"Better yet," Pete blurted, not wanting to be outdone, "we could *videotape* it and show parts during the presentation."

"Why don't we videotape the whole project? We can interview Mr. Whitehead, and videotape ourselves reading the report part of the project on location at the church."

"Great idea, Sidney!" Pete couldn't believe those words came out of his mouth. *Maybe Sidney isn't too bad after all,* Pete suddenly thought. "We could do it like a documentary. Hey, and maybe my dad will let us use his camcorder!"

"Since it's for school, I bet he would."

"All right!" Willy yelled. "Circus, here we come!"

For the next two weeks the boys had a lot of fun. Too much fun, they thought, to actually be working on homework. The hardest part of the project was deciding which parts of the church they wanted to talk about and which they wanted to keep secret.

And interviewing Pastor Whitehead turned out to be quite an experience.

"I've never been on TV before, boys," he said. "Is this going to make me a big star like Johnny Carson?"

"Grandpa," Jim replied, "this is just for our class. No one except Miss Vance and some eighth graders will see it."

"Well, you tell those kids that they can come over any time, and I'll sign autographs," he said, smiling. "Are you sure I look OK? You boys put on your Sunday best, and I don't even have on a necktie."

"Mr. Whitehead, we wanted to look like those documentaries we see in school and on PBS. The people interviewed are always wearing normal clothes, and the documentary guys are always in suits and ties."

Mr. Whitehead told about the history of the church: that it was built in 1758; that presidents Jefferson, Buchanan, both Roosevelts, and Carter visited the services; and that it was part of the Underground Railroad. After much debate, the boys even taped a section of the video in one of the tunnels that had been used to hide runaway slaves.

It took them two nights after school and a Saturday to finally record everything they needed. They went to the video shop near the Freeze, and Mr. Santini, the owner, helped them edit all their tape into an eight-minute documentary, complete with credits and a theme song. He even made a bloopers tape from all the leftover footage.

No one in class even came close to the gang's project, and they won the circus tickets hands down.

What happened at the circus, however, is a completely different adventure.

THE END

Turn to page 117.

Let's decide democratically," Pete said. "All those in favor of admitting Sidney into the group, raise your pencils."

Pete looked at Jim, who weakly raised his pencil. Then Pete continued the vote. "Those opposed, same sign." Immediately four pencils were waving in the air.

"Sorry, Jim," said Pete with a big grin, "but what makes this country so great is the voting system in which the majority decides an issue."

"I know how American politics work, but *you* had better get ready for a veto," snorted Jim.

Pete looked up and saw that Miss Vance was coming over to their group.

"I saw your hands raised. Did you have a question?"

"Um, uh . . . well, we, uh . . . no ma'am. No questions."

Chris tried to cover up Willy's smooth answer to Miss Vance. "We were just demonstrating the democratic process to our Brazilian friend."

"That's very admirable, boys," Miss Vance said, "but don't you think you should finish selecting members for your group? I see you still need one more member."

"Well," Chris started, "we actually did need to talk to you. We wanted to see if it would be OK if we could keep our group as is. We kind of like our own group, and we

56

really work great together. Adding another person could really throw us off. We want to maximize our full academic potential."

Even Pete was impressed with that last line. Surely that convinced Miss Vance. Just in case it didn't, he added, "Our cooperative skills will operate at optimum efficiency if you would allow us to work in our present unit."

The boys were sure that they would get their way. But their chins hit their desks when Miss Vance said in her Homey-the-Clown voice, "Miss Vance don't play dat. You have two choices. One, you can invite Sidney into your group and make him feel like one of this class. Or . . ."

"Or?" they all asked.

"Or, I invite Sidney into your group, making him feel unwanted and making you look selfish. But the choice is entirely up to you."

CHOICE ➡

If the Ringers now invite Sidney to the group, turn to page 38.

If Miss Vance makes the Ringers take Sidney, turn to page 96.

Chris was the first to start doodling, and then Sam and Willy followed. They didn't want to get in trouble, but Pete *was* their friend.

"OK, you young men may remain with Mr. Andersen after class. The rest of you use what little time there is left to start planning our projects. Jim, you can join this group," Miss Vance said as she pointed to the front left corner of the room. "Sidney, would you please move to the group at the back of your row."

When the bell rang, Pete, Chris, Sam, and Willy really got it. Because they refused to go along with the group selection, Miss Vance said that they would receive a zero for their project, "which constitutes a good part of your quarter grade." Miss Vance also made the guys sit in the vice-principal's office whenever the class worked on the projects.

And Miss Vance called their parents, who were not at all thrilled at the Ringers' behavior. Mrs. Washington couldn't believe that only Jim did what was right. She called the other Ringers' parents, and they all decided that they would ground the boys for a month and that each Ringer would take a Saturday and help Pastor Whitehead clean the church. And because they were grounded, they missed the circus that came to town.

58

Once they finally got paroled, they met at the Freeze to celebrate their freedom.

"You guys won't believe what I read last night," Willy said as he finished polishing off Millersburg's first six-flavor, eleven-topping banana split. "It was Proverbs 11:2. It said, 'When pride comes, then comes disgrace.'"

"Gee, Willy," said Pete as he wiped hot fudge from his face, "why couldn't you have read that before we got into all this mess?"

He then wadded up his napkin and threw it at Willy, hitting him in the nose and leaving a fudge smudge. It was the first attack in the greatest napkin war the Freeze ever hosted.

THE END

To see what would have happened if they had listened to Miss Vance, turn to page 80.

Or, turn to page 117.

Yeah, right! If you wanna go back to a room with a dead guy, you can." Sam shuddered. "It's just too creepy for me."

"But we wanted a topic for our report, and this oughtta be a great story," Chris pointed out.

"What about if we have Mr. Whitehead investigate? Or maybe the police?" Sam suggested.

"Grandpa would go up there," said Jim. "After all, it is his church."

"Let's go ask him," Willy said as he headed back into the church. *I'm glad I don't have to go back up there,* he thought.

The rest of the guys followed Willy to Mr. Whitehead's office and told him about the skeleton.

"I've come across some strange things in this church over the years, but this takes the cake! I'll go look into this."

Mr. Whitehead took the flashlight from the office and climbed the stairs. He examined the skeleton when he reached the room. As soon as he saw it, he chuckled and returned downstairs.

"Who was it, Pastor?" Sidney asked as soon as Mr. Whitehead returned to the office.

"Do you boys remember Old Doc Vaughn? Of course you wouldn't. He died years ago. Perhaps some of your parents will remember him. Well—"

"Was that Old Doc Vaughn?" Chris asked with a

60

gruesome expression, pointing to the floor above. The thought that the skeleton had once been a real live person gave him the chills.

"No, it's not Old Doc Vaughn." Mr. Whitehead chuckled. "He tutored medical students here at the church back when I was a boy, and he kept that up until he died—I guess that was about thirty years ago. What you boys have stumbled across here is his old medical skeleton."

"You mean like 'Mr. Bones' in Dr. Davis's office?" asked Jim.

"Yep! Just like it."

"Man, I'm glad we didn't call the police. They would've laughed at us big time," Chris said, greatly relieved.

"But this does show you, Sidney," Jim said, "that we never know what we'll find when we snoop around here. Maybe we can still find something to use for our project."

"I'm beginning to believe you," Sidney replied. "I just hope it isn't as scary as that skeleton."

THE END

If Sidney wants to continue this adventure, turn back to page 30 and make different choices along the way.

Otherwise, turn to page 117.

The Ringers and Sidney all nodded. "Make sure he doesn't know what you're doing," instructed Sam.

Officer Gary shot Sam a don't-tell-me-how-to-do-my-job look. "Don't worry. I'm a professional. I'll be back in a few minutes. In the meantime, wait here and stay out of trouble." With that he headed down to the chief's office.

"What do you think he's gonna find out?" Pete asked.

"Maybe the senator's son is a shoplifter," Chris offered.

"He must be pretty *strong,*" Sam said, causing the other guys to groan.

"What if he's on drugs?" asked Sidney. "That would really hurt the senator's campaign if anyone found out."

"Yeah," Chris agreed, "but it would make an *ex*-cellent report."

The next several minutes were spent with each Ringer imagining what Senator Lee's son did, what the senator offered Chief Brown, and what the circus would be like when they went with the tickets they'd win for exposing the scheme.

The sound of the door closing shook the guys out of their daydreams. Officer Gary returned and was motioning them to huddle in close.

"I've got a surprise for you. Do you wanna hear it?" The Ringers' eager expressions told Officer Gary to continue. "I saw Chief Brown, and he volunteered all the information to me about what you heard. I really can't tell you the details, but it's nothing like you were thinking." He paused, looking at the long faces of the gang. "I kind of figured," he continued, "that you'd react this way, so that's why I arranged this surprise. It may not be as sensational as corruption, but it should be good enough to get you an *A* on your project. Gentlemen," Officer Gary said as he opened the door, "I am pleased to introduce to you . . . Senator William Lee!"

Senator Lee entered the conference room and shook hands with each of the boys.

"The senator has fifteen minutes before he must leave for his next campaign stop, and he has agreed to be interviewed for your project."

"All right! Thanks, Senator," Willy said.

"I've got a question, Senator." Pete immediately said. "When you're in the Senate . . ."

The project was a success. Nobody else was even able to come close to an interview with a senator, so the gang won the circus tickets.

Pete even got to like Sidney. While they had been working on the report, Pete came to like the idea of having another "brain" around—it gave them a better chance at winning. *I'd hate to compete against a group Sidney's in,* Pete had thought more than once during the few weeks they were working together.

THE END

If you want to find out more about Senator Lee's son and his antics, turn back to the beginning and make different choices along the way.

Or, turn to page 117.

Miss Vance totally blew a gasket. This was her first year teaching, and she was not about to let her students get the better of her. Her face turned red as she commanded with a voice that was just short of a scream, "Mr. Andersen, you get yourself over to Sidney and Jim this *instant!*"

Pete flinched. He had never done anything like this before. Pete, the straight-*A*, mild-mannered rocket scientist, never disobeyed a teacher.

But if he gave in, he'd look like a first-class geek. Not really understanding why, he swallowed hard and just sat at his desk and started doodling. The other guys stared at him in disbelief.

Miss Vance clenched her fists at her side. "Mr. Andersen, you will stay after class. We have some business to settle." Then, looking at Sam, Chris, and Willy, Miss Vance asked in a measured voice, "Would you gentlemen join Sidney?"

Her request was most definitely an order, but the guys didn't know what to do. Sam looked at Willy, who looked at Chris, who looked at Sam, and then they all turned to Pete. They couldn't just bail out on their friend. But if they stuck together, they would be in deep trouble.

Whatever they did, they would have to decide quickly. Miss Vance was now rapping on the side of her desk with her fingers.

Every face in the class was fixed on the Ringers. Willy, Sam, and Chris were looking to Pete for some clue of what to do. In desperation, he shot them a look that said, "If you guys leave me here alone, I'll never speak to you again."

CHOICE

If Sam, Willy, and Chris stick with Pete, turn to page 57.

If the guys abandon Pete, turn to page 5.

66

Hold it, guys. Let's not chance him getting away before Officer Gary gets here," Chris advised. "If he hears you, he'll take off. Sam, why don't you try to get a shot from here, and Willy and Pete, you guys go around the front of the stores and wait at the other end of the alley. That way if he tries to escape, you two can stop him."

"Yeah, that's a good one, Chris," snorted Pete. "Us against that big kid?"

"Ah'll stop him," Willy said, doing his famous Arnold Schwarzenegger imitation. "He's no mahtch for da Terminator."

"You look more like the Geekinator," Sam teased.

"Get going, guys. Officer Gary should be here any minute," said Chris.

"We'll be bahck," Willy mechanically said as he headed to his post. Pete followed, shaking his head.

"I'm taking some pictures now, OK?" Sam asked Chris.

"Yeah, but don't let him see you. I'll look out for Jim and Officer Gary. Let me know if he starts hitting her or anything."

"There's no way I'd stay here if that happened," Sam said, the anger obvious in his voice.

As Sam took pictures, Roger kept struggling with the girl, but now he had a smile on his face. *Maybe he'll let her go now,* hoped Sam. But instead of letting her go, Roger pulled her close and kissed her. Sam turned to tell Chris, but just then saw Officer Gary's car pull up to the curb.

When he got out, Officer Gary walked up to Chris and Sam and said, "Thanks for watching the situation for me. I'll take it from here." He started down the alley and called, "Hey! What's goin' on down there?"

Roger Lee froze. The girl broke free and ran to Officer Gary. When she reached him, he said something to her quietly and pointed her in the direction of Jim and the guys.

"Kid, why don't you come over here. I need to ask you a few questions," Gary yelled to Roger.

Roger knew he was in trouble, so he took off running to the other end of the alley, hoping to get away from Officer Gary.

By this time Willy and Pete had just reached the other end of the alley. Now they looked and saw Roger and Officer Gary running right at them.

"Yikes!" Pete shouted. "What are we gonna do?"

CHOICE ➤

If they decide to charge Roger, turn to page 101.

If they think it's probably better stay where they are, turn to page 87.

68

Instead of answering Officer Gary, Sam closed the conference room door. He motioned with his hand for the gang to come closer. "I've got some news, but it's pretty important," Sam whispered. "No one can breathe a word of this to anyone, OK?"

Everyone nodded agreement, except Officer Gary. He just looked at Sam skeptically.

"I'm serious, Officer Gary. If you're not going to keep this a secret, I can't tell you."

"C'mon, Sam. You know I can't promise that. Especially if it concerns the police department or someone's safety." The look in Sam's eyes pretty much gave Officer Gary the clue that it was something he needed to know. "How about this: You let me in on your big scoop, and if it's necessary, I'll only tell the people who need to know. Otherwise, no one hears a word from me."

"I guess that'll be all right. But you can't let anyone from our class know, because I think this will be the prize-winning project. No offense, Officer Gary. I'm sure 9-1-1 is a good topic, too. Well, here it is. Senator Lee is in Chief Brown's office, and—"

"And we ask him for an interview, right?" Pete asked, thinking he was a step ahead of Sam.

"Wrong, Brainiac," Sam said proudly. He was never able to outwit Pete, and he enjoyed this moment. "That would be a good idea if I didn't know something that was way cooler. As I was saying, Senator Lee is in the chief's office, and I heard him offering Chief Brown a bribe to make sure his son stays out of trouble."

The Ringers were stunned. *Chief Brown could never be bribed,* Chris thought. The other guys were thinking the same thing (except Sidney because he didn't even know who Chief Brown was) when Officer Gary surprised them all: He laughed. Not just a little chuckle or giggle, but a deep, loud laugh that echoed in the conference room and made his face red and his eyes water.

When the policeman finally caught his breath he said, "That's a good one, Sam. Your delivery was great! I almost thought you were serious. . . . Wait, you were serious, weren't you?"

"Serious as a heart attack. I heard them when I was . . . uh, getting a drink, yeah. Senator Lee was talking about his son and how he gets in trouble, then about new equipment for the station, then the chief agreed to help."

"Did you hear the whole conversation?" asked Officer Gary.

"Well, no," Sam answered, looking at the ground.

"Are you positive you heard Chief Brown accept a bribe?"

"Pretty sure. I mean, what else could it be?" asked Sam defensively.

"It could be anything. We can't be sure you heard what you think you heard. In the justice system—and in reporting, too—we have to be sure of the facts before we find anyone guilty. Remember that," Officer Gary advised the group.

"Then let's investigate to prove what Sam heard," Chris said. "I think we need to know if they're crooks."

"I agree, Chris," Officer Gary answered. "It's very important that you get to the truth. If the chief and the senator are guilty, our community and state deserve to know. And if they're innocent, you couldn't do a report that falsely accused anyone. Right?"

The Ringers all nodded.

"In order to find out, do you want me to go to Chief Brown's office and do some investigating?"

"That'd be great!" Sam said. "Can I come with you? You know, as an assistant. Kind of like Sherlock Holmes and Dr. Watson."

"Sam, you're more like Maxwell Smart than Holmes or Watson," teased Pete.

"Maxwell Smart? Who's that?" Willy asked.

"You know, the show 'Get Smart'—with Agents 86 and 99?" Pete was answered by blank stares and shrugs. "Don't you guys ever watch *cable?"*

"Hey, guys! Remember me?" Officer Gary interrupted. "Do you want me to snoop around for you or not?"

CHOICE ⇒

If the Ringers want Officer Gary to spy for them, turn to page 61.

If they want to try something else, turn to page 109.

When Jim returned, he was swinging a large, rusty key from a long chain. "Grandpa says this is the master key. It should open any door up here."

"Great! Try the door on the right," Chris directed.

"Whatever you say." Jim unlocked the door, turned the knob, and said, "OK. Follow me."

Opening the door, Jim marched into the room, but before he could take a second step he hit a brick wall. The Ringers, who had been right behind Jim, all plowed into him, giving Jim two unpleasant jolts. Everyone staggered back, staring in disbelief at the wall.

"Hey, Jim. Your grandpa better call the police— somebody stole a room."

Jim, holding his head, said, "Don't make me laugh, Sam. It hurts when I laugh—*Ouch!*"

Chris examined Jim's head. "Man, you've got a megabump on your forehead. We better get you home."

"What about our search for a report topic?" Jim asked.

"We can do that some other time. You need to get home so your grandma can put some ice on your head before it swells up like a pumpkin."

"That I'd like to see," joked Sam. "And Halloween is coming soon. . . ."

"Ha, ha—*Ouch!* Stop it, Sam."

So they left the church and headed to Doctor

72

Grandma. On their way, Sidney mused out loud, "That was cool—I've never been in a building like that before! Secret passageways . . . doors with no rooms behind them . . . I wonder if there are rooms with secret doors?"

THE END

Turn to page 117.

After pulling Roger up, Officer Gary put handcuffs on him, dragged him over to the squad car, and stuffed him in the backseat. He then went over to talk to the girl, who was crying on Sidney's shoulder. Officer Gary talked to her alone for a few minutes and then called to Sidney, "Hey! Can you do me a big favor? Why don't you walk Margaret home. I'm sure she would feel safer with someone to walk with."

"Sure, Officer, no problem," Sidney said. He walked up to Margaret, who put her hand on his arm as they left.

The Ringers started to make kissy sounds, but Officer Gary shot them one of those don't-you-even-think-about-it looks. *That's OK,* Chris thought, *we'll have all night to give Sidney grief.*

"Thanks a lot, guys. I don't know if I would have caught him if it weren't for your quick moves," Gary said to Willy and Pete. "The chief will be very interested in this."

"No!" Sam blurted out. "You're not going to tell Chief Brown about this, are you?"

"Sure. He's the chief—he has to know. Besides, don't you want him to know about your bravery?"

"But he's in on it!" *Oops!* Sam thought. *I shouldn't have said that.*

"What are you talking about? Guys, what's goin' on?"

"We—I mean, Sam overheard Chief Brown talking to

Roger's dad a few weeks ago, and, well . . ." Chris wasn't sure what to say next. What if Officer Gary was in on the deal, too?

Sam finished the sentence for Chris. "And I thought I heard the senator make a deal with Chief Brown. I didn't hear it all, but Chief Brown said he'd help the senator—"

Sam was cut off by a loud burst of laughter from Officer Gary. "You thought that—" He had to pause to laugh again. "That Chief Brown accepted a bribe—*ha! ha!*—to let the senator's son get away with breaking the law? That's a riot!"

"But what about the new station and police cars and stuff?" demanded Willy.

"We hear that every time someone's up for reelection."

Sam was still suspicious. "If the chief wasn't bribed, just what *did* he agree to?"

"I guess I can tell you, but you guys can't tell anyone else, OK?" The Ringers nodded. "Roger has been in some trouble in D.C., and his dad kept bailing him out. You know—throwing his weight around with the police there. The situations were getting worse and worse, so when Roger came here to live with his grandma, Senator Lee hoped to use some 'shock therapy' to put Roger back on track. So at the first sign of trouble, Chief Brown agreed to really let Roger have it. This should teach him a lesson."

"What happens next?" Jim asked.

"Well, I put those cuffs on pretty tight, and he's gonna have the worst ride of his life. We're going to 'charge' him with assault, kidnapping, attempting to resist arrest, and anything else I can think of on the way. We'll put him through the process—fingerprinting, mug shots, the works—then the chief will have his turn at 'interrogating' him. Then we'll stick him in a cell for a few hours until his dad gets here, and if he still acts tough," Officer Gary said, smiling, "Officer Cliff will go into the cell undercover to give Roger a taste of a prison roommate."

"Man," Willy said as he pictured Officer Cliff, who looks more like a mountain than a policeman. "If that don't fix Roger, I don't know what will."

"Oh no! If there was no bribery or anything, our report is sunk!"

"Calm down, Jim. What about the info I gave you about 9-1-1?"

"It was kinda boring, Officer Gary," Willy shyly said. "When Sam told us about the senator, we gave up on that. I guess we'll have to go back to the 9-1-1 thing."

Officer Gary smiled and said, "I think I can help you out. But you have to promise to one condition." After the Ringers nodded agreement, Gary said, "Meet me at the station in ten minutes. I gotta run Roger in. Does this look mean enough?" He scrunched up his face and narrowed his eyes.

"I'm glad I'm not Roger," Willy said, cringing.

On Friday the twenty-third the Ringers had an incredible report. The title was "Inside Our Jail: A Close-Up Look at the Millersburg Police Department." Officer Gary and the chief let the Ringers observe the process of 'booking' a criminal—Roger Lee. Sam even took pictures at the station. These plus the pictures Sam took at the alley of the whole arrest made a great poster for the class presentation. They had to blot out the faces of Roger and Margaret for privacy, though, which turned out great because it made the pictures look more dramatic. Of course they won the circus tickets and got an *A*-plus on the project.

Their day at the circus was great. The guys ate ice cream cones, corn dogs, cotton candy, and Sno-Kones—plus Willy had a few hot pretzels, too.

"C'mon. Let's go to the side show. I wanna see the world's strongest man!" This was Jim's first American circus, and he didn't want to miss anything.

"You're looking at him," Willy said as he flexed his arms above his head.

"He said the strongest man, not the lizard boy," Chris teased.

"Very funny. But you better hide. I heard one of the keepers say a monkey escaped. They might put *you* in a cage by mistake!"

Willy and Chris joked the whole afternoon, but Pete and Sidney didn't notice much of it. They stuck close together and became pretty good friends. When they left the circus, Jim asked Pete about his change in attitude.

"He's not too bad," Pete answered. "Besides, we brains have to stick together, right?"

THE END

Turn to page 117.

Wait!" said Jim, "if I can convince you why we should have Sidney work with us, will you ask him?"

"Go ahead and try," Pete taunted.

"OK. Reason one: The more people in our group, the less work each of us has to do, right?" The Ringers nodded. "Reason two: If he's as smart as he seems to be, we stand a better chance of winning the circus tickets if he's on our side. And we do want to win circus tickets, don't we?"

"You convinced me," Willy said. "Any time I can do less work and win something, I'm all for it."

"Yeah," Chris hesitantly agreed. "And he has only been here a couple of days. Maybe he just made a bad impression by happening to know everything."

"I don't want to work with him. If he's as smart as you think, he can't be any fun."

The gang looked at Pete, not believing what he just said.

"Pete, man, you're right. You're smart, and you're no fun to hang around with." Sam smiled at Pete.

"Well, guys . . . that's, um, different." Pete tried to argue, but he knew he was beaten. "OK, you ask him. But I don't have to like him."

Chris and Jim brought Sidney over to their group. After they sat down, Jim asked, "Where you from, Sidney?"

"West Point." Noticing the Ringers' impressed

expressions, Sidney continued. "My dad taught history there. He retired from the army and is writing a book now."

"Excellent!" Willy blurted out. "About what?"

"Battle strategies of the Revolutionary War. It's really interesting so far. Dad tells me at dinner what he's written. He's going to be teaching at the college here next semester, too."

"Is he cool?" asked Willy. "I mean, as a teacher."

"Yeah. He really gets into his lessons. Why?"

"My brother, Zeke, goes to Mason U, and he's looking for the easiest classes."

"Willy, my dad's classes aren't easy. At the Point the cadets called him 'Hard Knox.'"

"That doesn't sound like Zeke's type of class," Sam said. "He had to study for his last eye exam!"

The guys talked and joked for a few minutes until the bell rang.

As they walked out of class, Pete said, "We didn't even talk about the project. Shouldn't we at least discuss a few options so we can do some preliminary research?"

"Pete's right," Sidney agreed. "I want to make sure I keep up my grades. My dad is pretty fanatical about grades since he is a teacher and all."

"'Grades'? 'Preliminary research'? I can't believe what I'm hearing," snorted Chris as he threw his hands up in the air. "You are forgetting the most important part of this whole thing."

Chris looked at Willy, and they both shouted, "Circus tickets!"

"I want to win the tickets, too," Jim said enthusiastically. "I've never been to an American circus before."

"Man, they're awesome!" Sam chimed. "They've got wild animals and daredevils and—"

"And hot dogs and cotton candy and pretzels—"

"And a side show and an arcade and—"

"And pop and corn dogs and candy and ice cream and—"

"OK, Willy. We get the idea. Don't you ever think about anything except food?" joked Pete.

"Sometimes. Like right now I'm thinking that we better go somewhere and plan our report before we have to go home for dinner."

"There's food again," commented Pete.

"Where do you wanna go?" Chris asked. "I'm sure Willy wants to go to the Freeze. Any other suggestions?"

"How about the church?" offered Jim.

"A *church?*" Sidney said as he chuckled. "You guys hang around churches after school?"

"My grandfather reopened the church," Jim answered defensively. "And we've had some great adventures there, too."

"Yeah. It's really old, and it's got these hidden passages and stuff. It's a cool place to hang out," Sam added.

Chris said, "Sidney, since you're new, you decide. Where do you want to go hang out and talk?"

CHOICE ⇒

If Sidney chooses the Freeze, turn to page 86.

If Sidney wants to see the church, turn to page 30.

Pete looked to the other guys. He wanted to see if they would stay with him if he refused to move. But as he saw the Ringers, he suddenly remembered how they got their name. *Remember to be ringers,* echoed in his brain. *We're supposed to be ringers for Jesus. And I know Jesus wouldn't disobey his teacher.*

As much as he didn't want to do what he had to do next, he did it anyway. He got up from his desk and walked to the front of the class. When he got to Miss Vance's desk, he said, "I'm sorry, ma'am. I didn't mean to be such a pain." Then he sat down by Jim and Sidney.

Well, since Pete was the reason the other Ringers didn't move in the first place, Chris, Willy, and Sam saw no reason to remain on Miss Vance's garbage list. They got up and hurriedly crossed the room.

A thin smile came to Miss Vance's lips. She had successfully handled her first crisis, and she was glad she didn't have to actually punish anyone. "OK, everyone, take the few minutes we have left to start planning."

As soon as those words were spoken, a dull humming of conversation began, with the kids discussing the Ringers' close call with the principal's office, the new movie showing at the Colonial Cinema, which girls liked which boys, which boys were avoiding which girls—anything *but* their projects. But the Ringers' group was silent. No one really knew what to say since there was an outsider with them, especially one who had caused so much trouble.

Jim was with Sidney the longest, so he felt it was his job to introduce the Ringers. "Sidney, these are my friends Willy, Chris, Sam, and Pete. I'm Jim."

Sidney mumbled a whisper of a hi that could barely be heard. The Ringers muttered some halfhearted hellos, except for Pete. He still wasn't thrilled about the idea of working with a competing whiz kid.

"Sidney, how did you know the answer to Miss Vance's question?" Once Jim asked the question, the other Ringers came to life. They had to know why this kid was so smart.

"Well," he said quietly, "my dad taught history at West Point. He has tons of books around the house, and on rainy days I sit and read them. And my dad took me on a tour of Civil War battle sites this past summer. I learned a lot then."

"Hey! You need to meet my cousin Jill. I bet you could stump her with some tricky history fact. I don't think she's ever been outdone when it comes to history." Even though Chris liked his cousin, he couldn't help but want to see her get something wrong for a change.

"Guys, the bell's gonna ring," Willy said. "Let's meet after school to plan our project. I want to go to the circus!"

"Why?" asked Sam. "Do you miss your old home?"

"No. I want to see if they'll take you. I hear they're short on clowns!"

Chris took control of the situation before they all got

82

yelled at for laughing in class. "Come on, guys. Should we go to the Freeze and work on our *award-winning* project?"

Sidney looked confused, then asked, "What's a freeze?"

"Not *a* freeze. *The* Freeze," Pete answered coldly. "It's just an ice cream place."

Willy couldn't believe Pete. "*Just* an ice cream place'? It's more than that—it's our hangout, and the ice cream there is incredible!"

For the first time today Sidney smiled. "I guess I could go for a double thick chocolate malt."

CHOICE ⇉

Does ice cream sound good to you, too? Turn to page 115.

I've just been walking around, getting a drink of water and stuff," Sam answered Officer Gary, not looking him in the eyes. He really wanted to tell everyone, but what if he couldn't trust Officer Gary? *I'll tell the guys as soon as we leave,* Sam decided.

When their crash course in 9-1-1 ended, Sam was anxious to leave, but Pete asked about six million technical questions. The rest of the guys were standing and giving Pete looks that said, "Who cares? Let's get some ice cream." But Pete ignored them and went right on asking about microchips, wires, and stuff that sounded like it was right out of "Star Trek." Even Sidney, the kid the Ringers thought was an Einstein, was looking blankly at the wall, obviously lost.

Sam felt like he would burst. They were on the verge of a major adventure, and Pete was holding them up. Finally Pete stopped talking computers, and everyone was relieved—especially Officer Gary. For the last five minutes of their question session he'd had no idea of what Pete was talking about; he had just stood there and listened to Pete answer his own questions.

With great effort Sam managed to wait until they got to the Freeze and ordered triple-scoop sundaes before he filled the Ringers in on his adventure in the hallway. The Ringers remembered their run-in with a senator in

Washington, and they could hardly believe their ears now.

"Wow!" exclaimed Willy. "I can't wait to tell the police about this."

"What do you mean 'police'? The police are in on it, Sherlock," Pete said. "If we tell them, we could get in trouble, too."

"Pete's right," Jim agreed. "Besides, we don't really have any proof. We don't even know if Chief Brown and Senator Lee made any deal. Their conversation sounded suspicious, but suspicious doesn't mean they're doing anything wrong."

Chris voiced the question they all wanted an answer to: "What should we do?"

"How about . . . we follow the senator's son. If the police bail him out of trouble, . . . we know Sam is right," Sidney shyly offered.

The Ringers had forgotten about Sidney in all of the excitement, so his idea hit them like a semi truck. "Why didn't we think of that?" Chris and Willy shouted in stereo.

"That's a great idea, but how do we know who Roger Lee is?" Pete coolly asked Sidney. "Do we ask every kid at Thomas Jackson High if his father is Senator Lee? Or better yet, maybe we can get on the PA and ask him to come to the office so that a bunch of kids can see who he is so they can follow him around town. What about—"

Willy cut off Pete's rare sarcasm. "What about if I ask Zeke to point him out to us? Last night at dinner he said some of his friends met this kid whose dad was a senator. I bet it's the same one we're talking about."

"Yeah, there aren't many kids whose dad is a senator."

"But we still don't know if Chief Brown agreed to anything or if the senator *really* offered him a bribe. Besides, we've got curfews and a project that's due. And what are the chances we'd actually see anything?" Jim said more than asked.

"C'mon, guys, we can't *not* follow up on this," Sidney begged. "I thought this was going to be a boring town, but now something might be happening. I may not get another chance to do anything this exciting again!"

"Don't worry about that," Willy said, chuckling. "There's always excitement around us. Well, guys, what do we do? Do we follow Roger and maybe expose corrupt officials, or do we do our boring 9-1-1 project?" Willy yawned for effect.

CHOICE ➤

If the Ringers decide to follow Roger, turn to page 23.

If they drop the matter and go for the yawner, turn to page 42.

86

Sidney could hardly remember the last time he'd been in a church. The suggestion that they go there made him feel strange. These 'Ringers,' as they called themselves, seemed friendly, but he had never felt like such an outsider before. Suddenly he wondered if he had gotten in with a bunch of religious fanatics.

He decided to play it safe. "Why don't we go to the Freeze," he said. "Ice cream sounds good to me."

"All right! The Freeze it is!" said Willy.

Turn to page 115.

Um, I don't know!" Willy yelled back.

They watched Roger get closer, and an idea came to Pete. "Hey, let's turn this Dumpster sideways. That way he won't be able to run past us."

"What then?" asked Willy, but he started rolling the Dumpster for lack of a better plan.

Once the garbage container was in place, there was a space of about four feet for Roger to run through, and Willy and Pete waited in the gap looking like linebackers—small linebackers.

When Roger reached the guys, he put his shoulder down and plowed into Willy, sending him sprawling. Pete, however, hit Roger in the legs and managed to grab a gym shoe, causing him to tumble to the ground. Roger tried to get up, but Pete had tangled himself up in Roger's legs, making it impossible for either boy to rise quickly. Fortunately Officer Gary was close behind. He grabbed Roger by the jacket before he could escape.

CHOICE

Turn to page 73.

Sam was not about to get caught there, so he took off running down the hallway. He heard the door to Chief Brown's office creak open. Looking around, he saw the men's room door. Quickly he opened it and slipped inside.

With his heart beating like the drums in a heavy metal song, Sam whispered a quick prayer, "Jesus, please make sure that Chief Brown didn't see me. If I get out of this, I'll mind my own business and go back to the group. Amen."

After taking a few deep breaths to calm down, Sam put his ear to the door to find out if anyone was following him. Sam heard footsteps, and they were growing louder. Someone was coming toward the washroom.

Sam ran into one of the stalls and jumped up on the toilet so no one could see his feet. Suddenly the door opened, and then someone turned on a faucet. While Sam waited for this person to leave, he started processing the information he had overheard. *The senator's son in trouble, new equipment, the chief helping* . . . to Sam it all added up to a bribe. *Not another senator,* Sam said to himself. *Every time we see one, he turns out to be a crook!* After several minutes, the person at the sink was still there. Sam mustered some courage and peeked over the stall to see who was there.

With a sigh of relief Sam jumped down from the toilet seat and exited the stall. He said to the person at the sink,

"Did you get bored, too?"

Willy jumped. "You scared me, Sam! I thought the place was empty. Man, my pen exploded, and I got ink all over my hands and my notebook. Officer Gary made me come in here and wash up before I stained the chairs and stuff. What have you been doing? Hiding in here?"

"Yeah, sure. I've been in here the whole time waiting to ambush you. I rigged your pen to explode, and I arranged with Officer Gary to send you in here."

"Like you could ever pull off something that cool," Willy said laughing. "You're missing some interesting stuff. It got better once Officer Gary got past all that electronic mumbo-jumbo. Whatcha been doin'?"

Sam wanted to tell Willy about the senator and the bribe, but he didn't even know who the senator was. Besides, he did promise God he'd mind his own business. "I've just been walking around. Nothing much, really. C'mon. Let's get back to the room. I wanna hear about some cool rescues and shootouts and junk like that!"

When they returned to the room, Officer Gary filled the boys in on all the emergencies in the previous month. Since Millersburg is so small, there wasn't too much that was really exciting. There were two calls to the fire department to come and get Mrs. Peabody's cat out of a tree. And a little boy had gotten his head stuck in a railing at the park when he was trying to reach a quarter he dropped.

When the class gave their presentations, the Ringers and Sidney did pretty well—they got an *A*-minus. They didn't win the tickets, though. A group of girls did a project on the town animal shelter, and they had pictures of puppies and kittens. And they had asked a volunteer from the shelter to come and tell about the animals that had been abused or abandoned. Oh well, the Ringers learned a valuable lesson about class reports: cute puppies are always worth a better grade than a kid with his head stuck in a railing.

THE END

The Ringers didn't win the circus tickets. But you can go back to the beginning and see if they didn't do better with other project choices.

Or, turn to page 117.

The looks on the Ringers' faces gave Officer Gary all the answer he needed. Jim and Sam raised their eyebrows and shrugged their shoulders. Chris and Willy wrinkled their noses and made faces. Pete and Sidney liked the idea but didn't say they did when they saw the others.

"OK, guys. You don't have to look so thrilled. If you change your mind, I'll be available. See ya later!"

Turn to page 43.

That's a good idea, 007. We can hide behind these Dumpsters as we close in. You got your camera ready?" Pete asked nervously.

"Yeah, it's all ready to shoot. But I don't have a pop can that conceals a tape recorder or any gadgets like that, Q, so you'll have to listen good."

"Of course. Let's get going, Bond."

"I don't know when Officer Gary's gonna get here, so you guys keep real quiet, OK? Willy," Chris ordered, turning to his best friend, "you go around the front of these stores and wait at the other side of the alley. You can stop him from running away if he sees Pete and Sam."

"Who? *Me?* Stop *him?* Maybe if he sees me there and doubles over laughing at the idea of me stopping him!" Seeing that Chris wasn't amused at the humor of the situation, Willy began his long walk to the other end of the alley.

"C'mon, Q, let's go," Sam commanded and headed toward Roger and the captive girl. They stalked quietly while behind one Dumpster and then tiptoed quickly to the next. When they got about fifteen feet from the pair, they could hear Roger's voice.

"Stop squirmin'. I'll let you go as soon as you give me a kiss!"

The girl was about to scream out again, so Roger

covered her mouth with his hand.

"Quit yellin'. C'mon, we both know you like me. So stop pretending you don't and kiss me!"

Roger lifted his hand from the girl's mouth and forced a kiss. She started hitting his shoulders and chest, and that was the picture Sam figured would be proof positive of the event. He lifted his camera, lined up the shot, and pressed the shutter. He got the picture, but the *whir* of his automatic winder was just a little too loud. Roger looked up and saw Sam's camera sneak back behind the Dumpster.

"Hey, you!" he shouted. "Come out here where I can see you!"

"Pete?" Sam said, the obvious question unspoken.

"I suggest we run like crazy!"

And so they did. There was total confusion for the next several seconds. Sam and Pete, obviously *not* role-playing anymore, came running back toward Chris, who was waiting at the corner, too surprised to move. Roger let go of the girl, started after the Ringers, then stopped and turned back to the girl again. Then he decided to let the girl go and get the camera, so again he ran after the Ringers. By this time Willy had reached the other end of the alley, having expected Roger to run at him; so when he saw everyone running the other way, he didn't know what to do. *Is it my breath?* he joked to himself. Finally he figured out that he should make sure the girl was OK, so he hurried down the alley to her. The girl wasn't confused at all: she knew that crying was the thing she should do.

Pete and Sam made it out to the street, with Roger close behind them. But as Roger rounded the corner to follow the guys, he ran into a big blue uniform. Officer Gary had just walked from his car with Jim and Sidney and was almost as surprised to have Roger crash into him as Roger was.

Officer Gary grabbed Roger and said, "These boys say there's been some trouble. What have you got to say about it?"

"Hey, man! I ain't done nothin' wrong. These kids were buggin' me, so I scared 'em away."

"That's not true, Officer Gary," Sam said, still gasping for breath from running. "I got a picture of him making that girl kiss him." Sam pointed down the alley toward Willy, who was walking over with the girl.

When they were close enough, Officer Gary asked the girl, "Miss, can you tell me what happened?"

"Yes, sir," she whispered, still sniffling and sobbing. "I was walking home . . . and . . . and he grabbed me . . . and forced me to go back there, and he . . . he tried to kiss me . . . and I don't . . . know what would have happened if these guys hadn't come to my rescue. . . . "

"Miss, why don't you sit on this bench here and try to calm down." Officer Gary motioned for Willy to guide her to the bench. "Now you," he growled at Roger, "up against that wall and assume the position. You're under arrest for assault, kidnapping, attempted assault, and lying to a police officer."

"You can't do this to me, man! I'm Senator Lee's son! Wait till my dad hears about this!"

"So you're Lee's son. I've heard about you, you punk. My chief is sure going to want to question you. But until we get to the station, these are for you to wear." Gary put the handcuffs on Roger and then read him his rights.

The Ringers and Sidney looked at each other in horror. *Not Chief Brown!* Sam thought. *He'll let this kid go.* Once Officer Gary got Roger loaded into the squad car, the Ringers pulled him aside.

"You can't let Chief Brown in on this! He'll . . . he'll—"

"Don't you guys worry. I know what's going on. Trust me on this, OK? Why don't you walk the young lady over to the station. I'll be there in a few minutes. I've got to have a talk with Roger first. Go on now."

Turn to page 21.

No one spoke.

"I'm waiting, boys. Which will it be?" Miss Vance pressed, looking down at them over her glasses as only teachers can do.

Jim started to answer, but then he stopped when he saw that the other Ringers were staring at him. The gang sat there, saying nothing, for what seemed like six and a half hours. No one wanted to disobey Miss Vance, but this strange force wouldn't let them ask Sidney to join them.

"Is this your final answer?" asked Miss Vance.

The boys just looked at the floor.

"OK. If that's the way you want it," Miss Vance said as she started walking to the front of the classroom. "Listen up, class! We seem to have three complete groups and one that needs some help. Sidney is all set, but the rest of his team is straggling. Let's see . . . Jim, why don't you come up here to the front and join Sidney?"

Jim's face turned red. He slowly gathered his books, looked at the Ringers, shrugged his shoulders, and started over to Sidney's desk. Throughout the class there were giggles, snickers, and some applause. *Yeah,* Jim thought, *Miss Vance sure knows where to hurt a guy—right in his ego!*

Once Jim made his humiliating trek across the room and sat down next to Sidney, Miss Vance called for Pete to come next.

I'm not going to let them laugh at me, too, thought Pete. *I'd rather eat a peanut butter and octopus sandwich.*

Miss Vance called him again. With the whole class staring at him, Pete sat still. Nothing Miss Vance could do to him would make him work with that know-it-all, Sidney.

CHOICE

If Pete refuses to move, turn to page 64.

If Pete changes his mind and obeys Miss Vance, turn to page 80.

Sidney didn't move.

As he hesitated, a man sitting in a booth on the opposite side of the Freeze got up and approached Pete. "Mr. Andersen, are you choking?" the coached asked.

Pete moved his head up and down, still grabbing his throat.

"Do exactly what I tell you. Stand up and try to relax." Pete stood up quickly, and Mr. Jennings turned Pete around so Pete's back was to him. He wrapped his arms around Pete, just under his ribcage, and said, "Try to relax."

As he said that, he tightened his arms and jerked Pete upward four times. At the fourth effort Pete let out a loud cough, and a chunk of banana and some ice cream shot out of his mouth.

Mr. Jennings helped Pete back into his seat and wiped his face with a napkin. "Mr. Washington, get your friend a glass of water."

Willy ran to the counter and called to Betty, who was in the back room, "Betty! Pete needs a glass of water. He almost choked to death."

Immediately Betty ran out to Willy. "What? Choked? Let me give him that water." She drew a glass of water from the tap and then ran over to Pete. "Here you go, you poor guy. Are you all right?"

Pete took a long drink before he answered. "Yeah,

thanks to Coach Jennings. Thank you, sir."

"You're lucky I was here. Who knows what would have happened. . . . Just make sure you chew better next time. Betty makes some great sundaes—slow down and enjoy them. See you gentlemen in class Monday."

After Coach Jennings went back to his table, Chris said to the guys, "I never thought I'd need to know anything like CPR or the Heimlich maneuver."

"Me either," Jim said. "I can't wait for that unit to come up in health class next semester."

Sidney sank down in his seat. *I should've tried to help. Why was I so scared to try?* Then he sat up and said, "I'm glad you're OK, Pete. I gotta go, you guys, but I'll try to think of something for our project. See ya in school." He stood up and quickly walked out of the Freeze.

"What's wrong with him?" asked Sam. "He didn't finish his banana split."

"Do you blame him? Pete was pretty disgusting," Chris joked, looking down at the mess Betty was cleaning up.

"I'm sorry. Next time I'll try to die neater."

The Ringers didn't see Sidney again until Monday. By then they had forgotten about Pete's brush with death, and their main concern was getting started on their project— whatever it turned out to be! Sidney was soon accepted by the guys and was treated almost like one of the gang. And his work on the project sure helped them avoid making it into a total fiasco.

100

THE END

To find out what the Ringers did for their project, turn back to page 30.

Or, turn to page 117.

What do you mean, 'What are we gonna do?' Let's get him!" yelled Willy.

Pete shrugged, said OK, and charged right at Roger. Willy was behind Pete, hoping to get a chance at Roger if Pete missed the tackle. *After playing football with Pete,* Willy thought, *I better be ready, 'cause Pete ain't no—*

"Oomph!" Pete and Roger collided, but Pete just bounced off him. Willy, however, instead of trying to grab Roger, dove into him, taking out Roger's legs. By the time Roger was able to scramble back to his feet, Officer Gary had him firmly by the collar of his jacket.

CHOICE

Turn to page 73.

I hate to say this," Pete said, "but Sidney's probably right. I mean, Indiana Jones wouldn't keep anything. He'd give it to the university he teaches at."

Sam's face brightened. "Sidney, didn't you say your dad's gonna teach at Mason U? We could give this stuff to the history museum there."

"And maybe there's something here that he could use in his book," Jim said.

Chris suggested, "We could even get our names on a plaque by the stuff. You know, 'From the Collection of . . .'"

"Are you guys sure about this?"

"Sure, Sidney," answered Willy. "Maybe your dad and Pastor Whitehead can come down tomorrow and check it all out. We could still use this stuff in our report though, right?"

"Yeah. We'll work it out with Sidney's dad." Chris took the blanket and threw it over the military items. "Let's go and tell your grandpa, Jim, and your dad, Sidney. Then let's figure out what we're gonna say in our report."

The next day, Sidney's dad accompanied the gang to the "traitor's room," as it came to be known by the Ringers. He was thrilled and surprised that everything was in good condition. After examining the find, he went upstairs and called Dr. Pennington, his boss and head of the history department at George Mason University.

Dr. Pennington arrived a half hour later. He recorded interviews with the guys about how they came across their discovery, and, using a special video-camera light, he videotaped the whole room, including the note on the door and even the arrow in the hallway wall.

Before they started loading Dr. Pennington's van, the Ringers took their own pictures of everything and found out what some of the more unusual objects were used for. Dr. Pennington even agreed to help them with their report on the finds—the letter from Benedict Arnold, the saber, the saddlebags, and the all-metal flintlock pistols that were found in the saddlebags.

When it came time for the reports, all the kids were blown away by the Ringers' and Sidney's project. Nobody else brought in a historian or an "archaeological find," as Dr. Pennington called the Revolutionary War artifacts. Of course they got an *A*-plus and won the circus tickets.

When Miss Vance gave them their tickets, they were all excited, but Willy was preoccupied.

"What's the matter?" asked Chris.

"I just thought of something scary. I actually liked this history stuff. I can understand now why Jill finds it so interesting."

"Oh no! You're turning into my cousin!" Chris covered his face in mock horror.

"I'm serious. Finding out about Benedict Arnold and the Revolution was cool. And did you see everyone's faces when they saw our stuff? They thought it was excellent. I think I want to be an archaeologist when I get older. It'd be fun to find all those old things."

"An archaeologist, huh?" Chris thought for a second. "I can *dig* that!"

They all groaned, even Sam.

THE END

Turn to page 117.

As Pete's expression got more frantic, Sidney felt more like he should do something. *I don't remember exactly what to do, but if I don't do anything, he could die.*

Before he really decided to, Sidney found himself getting up and moving toward Pete. "Stand up, Pete, and lean over the back of your chair." After Pete did as he was told, Sidney checked to make sure that Pete's stomach was over the back of the chair. Then he said, "Here we go."

He pushed down hard on Pete's back four times, causing Pete to cough up a huge banana slice and some ice cream. Pete took several deep breaths and stood up.

"Thanks a lot, Sidney. You saved my life."

"To tell you the truth, Pete, I wasn't sure I remembered how to do it."

"Where did you learn the Heimlich maneuver?" Jim asked.

"In school last year. It was part of our health class."

"We're supposed to learn that and CPR in health next semester," Willy said. "Almost too late."

"Thanks again, Sidney—you're a real friend. I'm gonna go home now, guys. Can we work on our project tomorrow?"

"Sure, Pete," answered Chris. "Anyway, I don't really feel like finishing my ice cream." Chris looked down at Pete's chair. "That *was* kind of gross."

106

As they were all leaving, Betty called out to the boys. "Pete, are you OK?" Pete nodded yes. She said, "Sidney, you are a real hero. Next time you come in, anything you want is on the house."

"Thank you." Sidney smiled a big smile. "But I was just helping my friend."

When Sidney was walking home, he thought back on his first week in Millersburg. *I made some great friends, saved someone's life, and got free ice cream. I think I'll like it here.*

THE END

Turn to page 117.

Not me!" yelled Willy. "Last time we were down there I thought I saw a rat!"

"A rat? I hate those things," Sidney said. "My vote is for going up."

"OK." Sam gave in. "But if we don't see anything up there, then we scope out the basement."

The guys entered the foyer and stared at the large wooden doors that led to the sanctuary. Willy walked up and patted the lamb that was carved into one of the doors. He started to say something, but Pete shot him a look that froze Willy.

If I have to go around our church with "Superbrain," I'm going to decide which passages, if any, he sees, Pete thought. "C'mon, Sidney. Follow me," Pete said as he ran up the stairway.

Sidney followed, running quickly to keep up with Pete, who was taking the stairs two at a time. The other Ringers took their time.

Jim whispered to Chris, "We always go through the secret passages. Why did Pete go up the regular stairs?"

"I think it's because he doesn't like Sidney much. Otherwise he would have been showing off our discoveries."

When the Ringers finally made it to the top, they found Pete and Sidney waiting quietly by two closed doors.

108

"I was just telling Sidney that these are the rooms we haven't been in yet. That door there," Pete said, pointing down the hallway, "just goes to an old picture room."

"Which room should we try?" asked Sam.

"Both doors are locked, so I don't think we can try either room," Pete said.

"Unless my grandfather has keys for these doors," Jim said, heading back for the stairs. "I'll find him and see. You guys decide which room will get us an *A* on our project."

CHOICE

If they choose the door on the right, turn to page 71.

If they choose the door on the left, turn to page 32.

Actually, Officer Gary, I think we'd rather do the work ourselves," Chris answered.

Sidney agreed. "It is our project. It's only fair that we do the investigating."

"OK, if that's the way you want it, that's all right—"

Officer Gary was interrupted by a page for him to report to Chief Brown's office.

"Gotta go, guys. You can stay here and plan what you'll do, OK? I hope I won't be too long."

After Officer Gary left, the gang sat for a while and considered their options.

Finally Sam suggested, "I could stake out Chief Brown's office. Maybe hear something more."

"And no one's gonna ask you why you're camped out at his doorway, right?" asked Pete. "Why not something more obvious, like going in and *asking* Chief Brown."

"Well, Mr. Negativity," Willy snapped, "what do you think we should do?"

"I suggest we listen in on his office. I've been working on some stuff from an old transistor radio and a broken telephone, and I've turned them into a crude bug. It is rather large, though. . . ."

"We could follow Roger and see what kind of trouble he gets into," Sidney said. "Then if he gets off, we know—"

The turn of the doorknob stopped everyone. The

door slowly opened, and in walked Chief Brown. He stood in the doorway for several moments, then he walked into the room and firmly closed the door. The expression on his face turned from a blank stare to a weird smile.

"It's a pleasure to see you boys. Officer Gary and I were just talking about you."

All the guys stepped back from the chief and grouped together near the far corner of the conference room. Their faces were lined with worry, and their eyes were bugged out from fear.

The door opened again, but this time Officer Gary walked in. The Ringers smiled when they saw him, but their smiles soon disappeared when he stood next to Chief Brown and folded his arms.

"We were deciding," the chief continued, "what to do about you. We just can't let you go since you overheard my conversation with Senator Lee."

"You . . . can't?" asked Chris, barely able to speak.

"No, we can't. Can we, Mr. Gary?" Officer Gary smiled fiendishly. Chief Brown nodded to his accomplice and then said to the guys, "You see, you spoiled the secret the senator and I hoped to keep just between ourselves. And . . . ," the chief said, pausing dramatically, "we must make sure you do not tell anyone."

As Chief Brown stepped toward our heroes, they bunched together and backed into the corner. There was no escape!

"In order to ensure your silence, I've ordered Officer Gary to round you fellows up, load you into a squad car, and take you to . . ."

The Ringers imagined all kinds of horrible possible endings to the chief's sentence. *To the woods, where you'll never be seen again,* thought Willy. *To the state prison,* guessed Sidney. The other Ringers pictured even worse consequences.

They all trembled as it seemed like forever for Chief Brown to finish, ". . . to the Freeze for ice cream!"

The Freeze? The guys looked at one another to make sure they weren't crazy.

"The Freeze, sir?" Sam's voice cracked.

Chief Brown smiled, then started laughing. "Sure. Right, Officer Gary?"

Gary had been doing everything he could to keep a straight face. But now he burst into laughter. "Yes, sir. They do seem to be little confused."

"Guys," Sam said, "I think we've just been had." Finally he ventured a snicker, then the other Ringers laughed too when they realized they weren't going to be prison slaves.

When the chief finally stopped laughing, he said to the boys, "Seriously, gentlemen. We were just having some fun with you. You see, you overheard a confidential conversation. Everything is legal, but rather sensitive. I called Officer Gary to my office to enlist his help, and he told me about your interpretation of things. So I thought I'd come down here to clear things up.

"And I also asked Officer Gary to take you to the Freeze and buy you some ice cream—your reward for keeping this a secret. Is it a deal, men?"

The Ringers didn't need to think about it: free ice

112

cream always beats a cool report. *We can come up with another topic,* Pete thought.

"Sure, Chief," Chris answered. "But will we ever find out what's going on?"

"I can't promise anything, fellows. Maybe down the line. For now, enjoy your ice cream."

"Nooo problemo," said Willy.

THE END

If you haven't found out what the chief and the senator talked about, or if you want to know what the Ringers did their project on, turn back to the beginning and make different choices along the way.

Or, turn to page 117.

The old sports saying, "The best defense is a great offense," came to Sam's mind. Sam wasn't sure if he had it backwards or not, but it sure seemed like a great idea. So, not knowing what he was going to say and not really sure of what he heard, Sam knocked quickly on the door to Chief Brown's office.

The door flew open, and Chief Brown suddenly filled the doorway. His face was flushed, and he was scowling.

Before the chief had a chance to say anything, Sam said, "Chief Brown, sir? Um, I hope I'm not disturbing you. My friends and I are, um, doing a social studies report on 9-1-1, and I wanted to ask you about, uh, how it's doing."

Chief Brown seemed to relax when he heard Sam say that this was about a school project. "Well, son, I'd like to chat with you, but I'm in the middle of a meeting with Senator Lee."

The chief turned sideways so Sam could see the senator, who was sitting on the edge of his chair, looking incredibly nervous. He, too, seemed to relax when he saw a kid. "Hello, young man," Senator Lee said. "It's always a pleasure to meet one of the future leaders of our great state."

Sam thought, *Oh, get real!* But he did say, "It's very nice to meet you, Senator." It looked like neither man suspected that Sam had overheard their conversation, and

Sam wanted to get out of there fast. "I'm sorry to have bothered you. I'll be getting back to my group."

As Sam turned to leave, Chief Brown stopped him. "Young man!" Sam froze, petrified. "If you want to stop by Monday after school, I'll see if I can't squeeze in an interview with you, OK?"

"Uh, sure, that would be great," said Sam, enormously relieved. "Thank you, sir."

Sam hurried down the hallway, hoping that Chief Brown wasn't suspicious. When he came to the water fountain, Sam bent down and took a long drink. As he was slurping the water, he turned his head and looked at the chief's doorway. Chief Brown was still standing there, staring at Sam. When Sam finished, he wiped his mouth with his sleeve, smiled at the chief, then headed down the hallway back to the conference room.

Officer Gary was talking about the dispatching of the police or fire department when Sam snuck back into the room. When he reached an appropriate stopping point, Officer Gary turned to Sam and asked, "Where you been, buddy?"

CHOICE ⇒

Does Sam tell everyone what he overheard? If so, turn to page 68.

If Sam waits to fill the Ringers in, turn to page 83.

The Ringers and Sidney got their jackets from their lockers and headed over to the Freeze.

Just as the gang started down Main Street, a police car drove up alongside them and the officer yelled out, "Hey, you kids! You look like you're out to make some trouble!"

Sidney jumped. The Ringers just smiled.

Willy yelled back, "Yeah, Officer Gary, we plan to do some serious damage to some of Betty's ice cream sundaes!" They all ran over to his squad car and gathered around the driver's side.

"We have to plan a social studies project," Sam explained. "Something about community awareness. So we were going over to the Freeze to try and come up with something."

"Well, I've got the rest of the day off. Why don't you guys pile into the squad car, and I'll take you to the station and show you how our emergency system works."

"That sounds really exciting," Chris said sarcastically. "After that we can sit in the Common and watch the leaves fall off the trees."

"That's real funny, Martin. Almost as funny as your batting average." Officer Gary coached Willy and Chris's baseball team, so he was pretty close to the guys. "Maybe your friends would find it interesting to know what happens whenever someone dials 9-1-1. How about it, guys?"

116

CHOICE ⇛

If the gang decides to go with Officer Gary, turn to page 11.

If the gang decides to go with Officer Gary, turn to page 11.

If they continue on their way to the Freeze, turn to page 91.

A simple homework assignment held some big
surprises for the Ringers and for Sidney, too. They also got
into trouble along the way. If you haven't found out about
all their discoveries, or about who won the circus tickets,
turn back to the beginning and make different choices
along the way to find out!

Also, be sure to read the other adventures of the
Ringers—Chris, Willy, Jill, Sam, Pete, Jim, and Tina. You
may even decide to become a Ringer, too!

Rick Blanchette is an assistant Bible editor at Tyndale House Publishers, Inc. He has served as a Sunday school teacher and youth leader in his church and was a contributor to *Who's Who in Christian History* (Tyndale).